STRANGE HAPPENINGS

STRANGE

HAPPENINGS

Five Tales
of
Transformation

AVI

HARCOURT, INC.

Orlando Austin New York San Diego Toronto London

www.HarcourtBooks.com

Library of Congress Cataloging-in-Publication Data
Avi, 1937–
Strange happenings: five tales of transformation/Avi.
p. cm.
Summary: Five original stories where strange changes occur,
from a boy and a cat changing places and a young man learning
the price of selfishness to an invisible princess finding herself.
1. Children's stories, American. 2. Metamorphosis—Juvenile fiction.
[1. Metamorphosis—Fiction. 2. Short stories.] I. Title.
PZ7.A953Str 2006
[Fic]—dc22 2004029579
ISBN-13: 978-0-15-205790-9 ISBN-10: 0-15-205790-0

Text set in Bembo
Designed by April Ward

First edition
A C E G H F D B

Printed in the United States of America

For Carolyn Shute

STRANGE HAPPENINGS

BORED TOM

AT THE AGE OF TWELVE, Thomas Osborn Pitzhugh—better known as Tom—had few interests, little desire, and almost no energy. This was so despite a family—mother, father, older brother, and sister—that loved him. As for school, his teachers treated him fairly; he did what he was supposed to do and received passable grades. But if you were to ask Tom what the future held for him, he would have replied that, other than getting older, and hopefully taller, he expected no change. In short, Thomas Osborn Pitzhugh—better known as Tom— found life *boring*.

One day Tom was sitting on the front steps of his city house doing what he usually did: nothing. As he sat there a short-haired, black-and-gray cat with gray eyes approached and sat down in front of him. For a while the two—boy and cat—stared at each other.

The cat spoke first. "What's happening?" he asked.

"Not much," Tom replied.

"Doing anything?" the cat asked.

"Nope."

"Just hanging out?"

"I guess."

"That something you do often?"

"Yeah."

"How come?" the cat inquired.

"I'm bored."

The cat considered this remark and then said, "You look like my kind of friend. How about adopting me?"

"Why should I?"

"Got anything better to do?"

"I don't know."

"Well then?"

Tom asked, "What's your name?"

"Charley."

"Okay."

It was not long before Charley the cat became part of Tom's household. So familiar did he become that when Tom went to sleep, Charley slept next to his head on an extra pillow.

For a brief time, Tom—having a new friend—was almost not bored. After a while, however, his life settled back into its old, boring routine.

"Hey, man," Tom said to Charley one afternoon two months after the cat had moved in. "It's not fair! You get to sleep all day, but I have to go to school." Disgusted, he flung his schoolbooks onto his bed.

It was the statement more than the *thump* of books that awoke Charley from a sound nap. He studied Tom, and then stretched his back to curve like a McDonald's arch. "I am a cat," he said. "You are a boy. Some would say you had it better."

Tom sighed. "If you had to go to school every day like I do, you wouldn't say that."

3

"Don't you like school?" Charley asked.

"Oh, I like it all right," Tom replied. "The kids are okay. The teachers are all right. Once in a while it almost gets interesting. Mostly, though, it's just boring. I'd rather do nothing. Like you."

"What about after school?"

"*Boring*," Tom insisted.

"Doesn't *anything* interest you?"

Tom considered the question. "Television," he said at last. "On TV there's something happening. It's my life that's dull."

"A cat's life," said Charley, "can be dull, too."

"Your life is supposed to be dull," Tom said. "See, people are *always* telling me that I should get up and *do* something. Boy, wish I had permission to sleep all day the way you do."

To which Charley said, "How about you becoming me, a cat, while I become you, a boy?"

Tom sighed with regret. "Not possible," he said.

"Don't be so sure," said Charley. "Most people wouldn't believe that you and I could hold a conversation, but here we are doing just that."

"Actually," said Tom, "it's not that interesting a conversation."

"Whatever you say," Charley replied as he curled himself into a ball, closed his eyes, and went back to sleep. Tom did pretty much the same: He watched television.

The next day Tom, as usual, went to school. In most ways school was ordinary. Although Mr. Oliver called upon him once and Tom gave a reasonable response, he never raised his hand. Most of the time he doodled, stared out the window, or daydreamed, but about what he could not have said.

At the end of that day, Mr. Oliver announced a special homework assignment. He asked each student to write an essay titled "The Most Exciting Thing That Ever Happened to Me." It was due in one week's time.

Tom was worried. He could not think of anything in his life that had been exciting. He did remember a family trip when they'd had a flat tire on the highway. That was not so much exciting as it was nerve-racking.

Then there was the time he was taken to a baseball game, but no one even got a hit until the bottom of the ninth inning.

Tom also recalled the time his mother had thought she might lose her job. That was scary, not exciting.

"You ever do anything exciting in your life?" Tom asked Charley when he got home.

Charley, who, as usual, had been sleeping on Tom's bed, stretched, yawned, and said, "As a cat?"

"Of course as a cat."

Charley said, "I caught a mouse once."

"Was that exciting?"

"It was just a small mouse. My first ever."

"What did you do with it?"

"Let it go."

"Anything else?"

"Since I've moved in here, I've caught a whiff of another cat passing through your backyard. I believe it's a cat of my acquaintance—her name is Maggie. She's in search of a home of her own."

"Is *that* exciting?"

"For a cat it can be hard," said Charley. "Why all these questions?"

Tom told Charley about the essay he had to write. "But," he complained, "nothing exciting has *ever* happened to me."

Charley thought for a while. "Tom," he said after a while, "do you remember what I told you—that you could become me and I could become you?"

"Yeah."

"You might find *that* exciting."

Tom smiled. "Sleeping all day with no one objecting sounds cool to me. Could it be done?"

"We can give it a shot," said Charley. "A few blocks from here there's a neighborhood wizard-cat. It's that Maggie I just mentioned. We could ask her."

"Just remember," Tom warned, "if we make the change, you'll have to write that essay. It's due next week."

"I know. And you'll get to sleep all day."

"Sounds good to me," Tom said. "Anyway, we could do it just long enough for you to write my essay."

Charley, ignoring *that* remark, said, "Let's make the change now."

"*Now?*" said Tom. He was not given to making quick decisions.

"Any reason not to?"

"Maybe my parents—"

"I'll handle them."

With Charlie leading the way, they left immediately.

It was dusk. A thin haze filled the air. Streetlamps began to flicker on. As it grew darker, people hurried to get home. Soon the streets were quite deserted. Tom was glad Charley knew the way.

They went two blocks to the right, one to the left, and then walked through a back alley Tom had never wanted to walk through. Finally they cut through a weed-and-bedspring-infested yard and approached what looked to Tom to be an abandoned building. Its windows were boarded. Tom hoped they would not be going there. But Charley, without a pause, padded into the building's basement and down a long empty corridor.

Tom, feeling nervous, said, "Do we have far to go?"

"Not too long," said Charley as he headed up a rickety flight of steps.

They reached the first floor. When Tom's eyes grew accustomed to the gloom, he realized that the building was full of cats. Some were sleeping. Others sat with tails curled about their feet, staring into the distance. A few prowled restlessly. Charley nodded—as if they were acquaintances.

With Charley leading the way, Tom entered a long, dimly lit hallway. Green paint peeled from the walls. The ceiling looked like it might collapse any moment. There were more cats. Some glanced at Tom, but most paid no attention.

At the end of the hallway was a door. In front of this door sat a large cat, the largest cat Tom had ever seen. He looked like a miniature tiger.

Charley approached this large cat with great respect. For a few moments the two cats stared at each other, their tails moving restlessly.

"What can we do for you?" said the large cat.

"A transformation," Charley said.

Tom saw the large cat's eyes shift to him, then turn back to Charley. "What's the reason?" the large cat asked.

"He's bored," Charley said. "And he has to write a school essay, 'The Most Exciting Thing That Ever Happened to Me.'"

"Ah! One of *those,*" the large cat said as if he had heard it before. "You can enter."

"Watch your head," Charley cautioned Tom.

Tom was just about to ask Charley if this kind of transformation was common, when they stepped into a small, dim room. The floor was so carpeted with cats, it was hard to move about. Some cats were big, others small. Some were perched on ledges. Others sat on shelves like books in a library. The whole room throbbed with such a steady purring, it was as if one low note on a bass guitar were being continually thrummed.

No matter where the cats sat or lay, all eyes were fixed upon a raised platform at the far end of the room. The platform was dimly lit by dusty light that drifted through a broken piece of window boarding.

On the platform, on a purple pillow, a gray cat lay stretched out, one cheek resting on an extended front paw. Her long fur made it appear as if she were dressed in silk lounging pajamas. Her eyes were closed to narrow slits. Now and again the tip of her tail shivered delicately.

"Who's that?" Tom asked Charley.

"Maggie," Charley whispered. "The local wizard-cat. Most neighborhoods have them. On the street she leads a normal life. Here, she's a wizard. Stay close and don't say anything unless you're asked a direct question."

Charley padded his way to the platform. Once there he lay down and tucked his front paws under his chest. "Kneel," he whispered.

Tom knelt.

"Now, be patient."

Tom, curious how a cat could have become a wizard, gazed at Maggie.

The gray cat finally looked up. "What's happening?" she asked. Her voice was small, delicate.

"Maggie," said Charley, "we're requesting a transformation. This boy—his name is Tom—and myself."

"Wants to be a regular *tom*cat, I suppose," Maggie said. Her silky sides heaved slightly as she enjoyed her joke.

"Actually," Charley explained, "he's bored. Wants to sleep all day, the way I do."

"Lucky you," Maggie murmured to Charley. With a sidelong glance at Tom, she asked, "*Do* you really want to sleep all day?"

It took a moment for Tom to realize he had been asked a question. "Absolutely," he replied. "I love to sleep."

Maggie sighed. "I'd settle for a decent home off the streets."

"I've got that," Tom said.

"Whatever," Maggie mumbled. Then she said, "Bow down. You need to have your heads close together."

Tom and Charley put their heads side by side.

Tom was not sure what happened next. He sensed that Maggie's tail curled around and batted him on the forehead. He supposed the same thing had happened to Charley.

The next moment he heard Maggie say, "Charley, enjoy that home of yours."

"Let's go," said Charley. Tom turned and sensed the room had grown much larger. What's more, he was staring—nose to nose—into the face of a large calico cat with curled whiskers. "Beg pardon," said Tom, as he sidestepped the cat.

He turned to see if Charley was there. What he saw was the leg of the largest human he had ever seen, a boy who towered so high into the room, Tom could not see his head.

Confused, Tom called, "Charley?"

"Right here," came a voice from the huge boy.

A shock ran through Tom from the tip of his nose leather to the tip of his tail. He understood: He had a tail because he'd become a cat. A cat that looked exactly like Charley, even as Charley now looked exactly like Tom.

They had exchanged bodies.

Tom lifted a hand in front of his face. It was a paw covered with black-and-gray fur. "Cool," he said. "I've become a cat."

"Let's go," Charley urged, and gave Tom a gentle spank on his rump to get him out the door.

Though Tom had spent his whole life in that neighborhood, going home was like traveling through a foreign county. Everything was gigantic. Even things he could recognize—like mailboxes—appeared to be twisted into odd shapes. What's more, he seemed to be at the bottom of a sea of smells. One moment he sensed something delicious to eat. The next moment he had a trembling aware-ness of danger that was almost instantly followed by a whiff of calm. That in turn was taken over by the delicate scent of friendship. Tom, who had never been aware of such smells, was astonished he could identify them so clearly.

Even more amazing was that his body felt so different. He had never thought much about having hands and feet, or a head, for that matter, unless he bumped himself. Now he felt loose and jangly, as though he were not tied together tightly. He was also very aware of his skin. Some spots felt so dirty he had a desire to lick them clean. Other places itched and were in need of scratching. He even had a desire to stretch out and flex his nails into something deep and soft, like a nice stuffed chair.

The only reason he didn't do all these things was because he was having trouble keeping up with Charley, who was striding along on long human legs.

"Come on, now. Don't dawdle," Charley kept saying. Tom, fearing he would not be able to get back home on his own, hurried.

They reached the house. Tom was about to open the door when he realized he could not do it. Charley did.

"Oh, there you are," came the familiar voice of Tom's father. "I was getting worried about where you were."

Tom answered. He said, "Charley and I went for a walk," but the only sound he heard was a meow.

"That cat seems to know," Tom's father said with a good-natured laugh. "Where were you?"

"Just hanging around the neighborhood," said Charley vaguely.

"Don't you have homework to do?"

"No problem. I just have to start writing an essay called 'The Most Exciting Thing That Ever Happened to Me.'"

"Interesting. What are you going to write about?"

"Don't know. But I'm really looking forward to it."

"Hey," said Tom's father, "I love to hear that enthusiasm for a change."

Tom, curling about Charley's feet, felt contented. "I'm going off to sleep," he announced. Charley reached down and gave Tom a reassuring scratch behind the ear.

Tom strolled over to his own bed, leaped up, found the cat's pillow, and closed his eyes. In moments he was asleep, purring gently.

Charley sat down to compose the essay.

———

During the next few days, all went well. Tom enjoyed doing nothing, sleeping all day on his own bed. Occasionally he slept in a different place. Once, he went for a stroll in the backyard.

Meanwhile, Charley lived Tom's life. He went to school. He played with Tom's friends. He enjoyed Tom's family.

On the fifth day Tom began to get restless. He was bored with just sleeping. He would have watched television, but he had to wait for others to turn the TV on, and they didn't always choose his favorite programs.

Twice, Tom started to read the daily newspapers only to be picked up and placed firmly in the litter box. He was not being understood.

Frustrated, Tom ventured onto the streets. Once there he narrowly avoided being hit by a car, had his tail pulled by an infant, was teased by an older child, and then was chased by a dog. By then he'd begun to think he'd had enough of being a cat. He took a nap.

That afternoon, when he got home from school, Charley put his schoolbooks down and said, "Today was not a good day!"

Tom awoke, yawned, stretched, and looked around. "What's the matter?"

"Remember that essay?"

"'The Most Exciting Thing That Ever Happened to Me'?"

"Exactly," Charley said. "You know how hard I worked on it. It was due today. When we got to the moment to share papers, I volunteered to read mine."

"Mr. Oliver must have been surprised."

"He sure was. I guess you never volunteered for anything."

"No way," Tom agreed.

"Anyway, he called on me and I read."

"What happened?"

Charley held up the pages he had written. "He said my work was a fine piece of writing, but he didn't want fiction. He wanted something *real*."

"What did you write about?"

"Transformation: 'How I, Once a Boy, Became a Cat.' Though the whole class liked it and Mr. Oliver admitted it was fun, he said I have to do the whole thing again. Make it real. But every word of it was true!" Disgusted, Charley threw his paper onto his desk.

Tom scratched himself beneath the chin. "You could write about that time you caught a mouse."

"Oh sure. As if he'd believe that," said Charley, and he went off in a huff.

Tom, reminding himself that he wanted to talk to Charley about going through the transformation process again, was just about to slip back into a nap when something Charley had said floated through his mind. What was it? Oh yes . . . did Charley say that the subject he had written about was, "*How I, Once a Boy, Became a Cat*"?

Surely what Charley meant to say was the other way around—that is, "How I, Once a Cat, Became a Boy." Or was he writing about how *he*, Tom, became a cat?

It was too confusing. Tom yawned and shut his eyes again. But he could not sleep. What Charley had said bothered him.

At last he got up and looked around for Charley, but the boy had gone out. Back in his room, Tom noticed that the paper Charley had written was lying on the desk.

He read it. It was just what Charley had said: a report about a boy who had turned into a cat. This boy, so Charley had written, wished to become a cat and sleep all the time. That was familiar enough. In fact, as Tom went through it, the whole story was his *own* experience. However, in Charley's story, the boy's name was Charley and the cat's name was Felix.

Why, Tom wondered, *would Charley have everything the same,* except *the names?*

"Hey, Charley," Tom said that night as Charley sat at the desk working on his new essay. "I read your essay."

Charley glanced around. He seemed surprised. "That's not like you."

"You left it out."

"Whatever. Did you . . . like it?"

"It was fine," said Tom. "It was pretty accurate, too. Except for two things."

"What's that?"

"You changed the names around. You called the boy Charley and the cat Felix."

"Oh, right," said Charley, turning back to his work.

"How come you did that?" Tom asked.

"It was supposed to be true," Charley muttered.

Tom frowned. "I don't follow."

Charley turned around to gaze at Tom evenly. "I guess there's no harm in telling you *now*."

"Telling what *now*?"

"Well, before I introduced myself to you and you took me in, I was once a boy, and my name was Charles."

"You *were*?"

"See, I was bored with my life—so bored, I began thinking that things would be better if I were a cat. As it turned out, I met a cat. Or rather, this cat

21

introduced himself to me. His name was Felix. Felix knew about one of these neighborhood wizard-cats. Sound familiar? You can guess the rest."

As Charley was telling this story, Tom felt increasingly troubled. "Charley," he said, "are you telling me—as you sit at *my* desk, wearing *my* clothes, doing *my* homework, looking like *me*—that at one time *you* were a boy and *then* became a cat? But then you decided you didn't want to be a cat and so became me instead?"

"You've got it."

"But . . . but why didn't you and that Felix just change back to what you were?"

"Felix didn't want to be a cat again."

"He didn't?"

"Nope."

"Charley, are you saying you found me and tricked me into—"

Tom interrupted, "It was what you wanted, too."

"But that's outrageous!" cried Tom. "Anyway," he said, "I've had enough of sleeping. I want to change back."

"Sorry," Charley said. "Too late for that."

Tom, who was becoming increasingly upset, stared at Charley. "What do you mean?"

"I prefer being a boy again. This is a great place and your family is nice." So saying, he left the room, shutting the door behind him.

At first Tom was too astounded to do anything. Then he leaped off the bed and headed right for the door, only to remember that he had to get a person to open it for him. He called to Charley, but it was not Charley who came. It was his mother.

"Want to go out?" she asked, reaching down and chucking Tom under the chin.

"Of course I want to go out," Tom said in a rather irritated way. But when he spoke, all his mother heard was caterwauling.

"Isn't it cute the way cats talk," she said as she scooped him up and set him gently but firmly out the front door. "Now go play."

An indignant Tom looked up and down the street. It was all very different since he had become a cat. He closed his eyes and breathed deeply, trying to sort out the many scents. Then he began to go toward what he hoped would be an audience with Maggie.

It took a while, but at last Tom found the abandoned building. Once again he went into the basement, then to the long, dimly lit hallway, passing through the multitude of cats. The large tiger cat sat in front of the doorway at the end of the hall.

"What can we do for you?" asked the large cat.

Tom said, "A transformation."

"With whom?"

"With the one I was transformed from."

"Is he here?"

"Well, no."

"Then forget it. Anyway, Maggie's out."

"Where?"

"Hey, pal, she has her own life."

"But . . ."

"Beat it, tomcat," snarled the large cat, and he hissed. Tom backed away and made his way home.

That night Tom had it out with Charley.

"The point is," Tom said hotly, "you weren't

being honest with me. In your paper you said you were a boy."

"I was."

"Then you became a cat, and now you're a boy again."

"All true."

"Now you say you have no desire to change back."

"I'm being honest, dude," said Charley. "Come on, you *wanted* to sleep all day, didn't you? Just lay about."

"I know. But that's more boring than staying awake."

"Hey, Tom, you made a deal. If you don't like it, go find another kid who is as bored with things as you were. Believe me, there are plenty of them. A lot of the cats at Maggie's used to be kids who were bored with their lives."

"Is that true?"

"Half the kids in your class used to be cats!"

Tom was shocked. "They were?"

"Trust me," said Charley. "You know the story:

Kids get bored. Want to sleep all day instead of going to school. Bingo! Kids become cats. Cats become kids. They're the lively ones, always raising their hands."

"But I want to be a *human*," Tom cried. "Not some cat!"

"Go find a kid to exchange with you. Now please, leave me in peace. I have to write this essay."

"But . . ."

Suddenly, Charley picked Tom up, and despite Tom's howl of protest, put him out of the room.

Tom slipped from the house through an open window. It was quite late, and the moon was large in the sky. He went around to the backyard, climbed the fence, and sniffed. The air was full of pungent smells. The only one he found interesting was the scent of his own home. It made his heart ache. Lifting his head, he let out a long piercing howl of misery. Then another.

A window opened. A voice growled, "Shut up, cat! I'm trying to sleep!"

A mournful Tom slunk out of the yard and onto

the street. A thousand distinct odors wafted through the air, a tapestry of smells too complex for Tom to untangle.

He wandered on, paying little attention to where he was going, up and down streets, through alleys, along back fences.

Tom had been walking for about an hour when he heard spitting and hissing. He stopped and listened. It was a catfight. He looked to see where it was coming from, spied an alley, and trotted over.

At the far end of the alley were two cats. One was a sleek brown Siamese, the other a gray cat. The gray one had been forced back against the fence by the Siamese.

"Help!" cried the gray cat. "Help!"

Hardly thinking of what he was doing, Tom let out a howl and dashed down the alley. The Siamese turned to confront him. Tom leaped over him and came down beside the gray cat. Tom hissed, showed his fangs, and raised a claw-extended paw.

The Siamese, confronted by two cats, backed off, turned, and fled.

"He's gone," Tom said, panting to catch his breath.

"Thank you," the gray cat replied.

Tom turned and looked at this other cat for the first time. "Hey, you're Maggie, the wizard-cat!" he cried.

"Do I know you?" said Maggie.

"My name is Tom. You transformed me from a boy. The cat was named Charley."

"I'm sorry. I can't remember. These transformations come by the litter. After a while all you people look alike."

"We do?"

"A certain blandness. No show of emotion. As if you can't bother. So, sorry, I don't remember you. But I'm ever so grateful. If I can return the favor . . ."

"Oh, but you can," Tom said eagerly.

"How's that?"

"Transform me back."

"To what you were?"

"Right."

"How does the other one—the one I transformed you with—feel?"

"I don't think he wants to switch."

"I'm afraid that's what usually happens. It makes retransformation nearly impossible."

"But you *can* do it, can't you?"

"Oh sure, but the point is, you have to get the two heads side by side. If one doesn't want to, and that one is a human, it isn't easy."

"I can arrange it!" Tom cried.

"How?"

"Follow me."

Tom led the way back to his own house. They reached it by two in the morning. Finding the window through which Tom had got out still open, they crawled inside.

Maggie looked about. "Nice place you got here," she muttered.

"*Shh,*" Tom whispered. He led the way to his room, and by standing up on his hind legs—Maggie helped—they were able to push the door open.

Charley, head upon a pillow, lay fast asleep on the bed.

"Now listen carefully," Tom said to Maggie, "I'll get on the pillow right next to him and put my head near his. Give me a minute. Then, you jump on and do what you normally do. Just make the transformation."

Maggie giggled. "Someone's going to be surprised."

"That's Charley's problem. He tricked me into this."

"That's what you all say," said Maggie.

Tom leaped onto the bed and padded to his own pillow. Once there he lay down, tucked his paws under his chest, and nestled his head right next to Charley's.

Within moments Maggie followed. "Ready?" she whispered.

"Ready," Tom replied.

"Here goes," Maggie warned.

Tom closed his eyes and waited for the tap on

his forehead. When nothing happened he opened his eyes and found himself staring right into the face of a gray cat.

Puzzled, Tom called, "Maggie?"

"The name's Charley," the cat said.

"*Charley?*" Tom cried, and looked down at himself. He was just the way he had been moments before—a cat. In a panic he turned. There, asleep, was a person who looked exactly like he had looked. As for the second cat, it looked just like Maggie.

"Hey," Charley—now Maggie—growled, "what's going on? How come I'm a cat again?"

"I'm afraid . . . Maggie did it," said Tom.

"Maggie? The wizard-cat?"

"I think so. She did the transformation on herself and you. She's become . . . *us.*"

One week later, Tom—who had spent all his time prowling the streets—suddenly stopped. He was in a park not far from a bench. Sitting on the bench was a girl. She was not doing anything in particular, just sitting. Now and again she swung a leg back and forth. Then she yawned, looked at her watch, and yawned again.

Tom watched her for about fifteen minutes. In all that time the girl continued to just sit there, a slight frown on her face. She looked bored.

Tom went forward and sat down in front of the girl.

"What's happening?" he said.

The girl looked down at him. After a moment she said, "Nothing."

"Doing anything?" asked Tom.

"Nothing *to* do," the girl replied.

"Bored?"

"Always."

Tom got up, stretched, and then rubbed himself against the girl's leg. "You sound like my kind of friend," he said.

BABETTE THE BEAUTIFUL

IN THE LAND OF SOLANDIA, it was a queen, not a
king, who ruled. Some years ago it was Queen Isabelle—*not* King Alfredo—who was the reigning
monarch. Hardly a surprise then that Isabelle wished
to give birth to a girl so that her daughter might
become the next queen. That said, the queen felt
strongly that any daughter of hers *must* be very
beautiful because she believed only beautiful girls
could be happy.

The truth is, Queen Isabelle thought about having a beautiful daughter *all* the time. If you asked—
and even if you did not ask—the queen could—and

would—tell you what this hoped-for daughter would look like. What's more, the queen could—and would—describe this daughter's beauty in great detail for hours at a time. She even knew her name: Babette. The queen chose the name because she wanted her daughter—when she became queen—to be known as—Babette the Beautiful.

Unfortunately, there was no child. And time was passing.

One day a lady-in-waiting told Queen Isabelle about an old woman who had recently arrived in the city. The woman's name was Esmeralda. Esmeralda—so the lady-in-waiting claimed—had powers to enable women to bear *exactly* the kind of child they desired.

When the queen expressed interest in this Esmeralda, the lady-in-waiting told the queen where the old woman lived.

Disguising herself—and telling no one where she was going—Queen Isabelle made her way to a dark alley in the oldest part of the old city. There she knocked on an ancient door. The door was opened by a little old woman with a twisted body. Her face was ugly, her hair sparse and gray. Her hands were gnarled, and ribboned with veins. Upon her frail shoulders lay a tattered blue-and-green shawl.

The queen, shocked by the woman's appearance, stepped back from the door. "I think I have made a mistake," she said, and turned to leave.

Before the queen could go three steps, the old woman cried: "Stay, Queen! I am Esmeralda, the only person who can help you to have the beautiful daughter you desire!"

The queen looked back at the woman. "How do you know who I am and what I wish?" she said.

"Because," said Esmeralda, "my powers are mirrors that reflect your desires."

"But how can you, who are so ugly," said the queen, "help me to have a beautiful daughter?"

Though she heard the insult, Esmeralda said only, "You must trust me."

Queen Isabelle laughed. "Do you really expect me to trust someone who is as hideous as you?"

Esmeralda's eyes gleamed with anger. "My queen,

I have a large mirror which I will place between us. You can talk to me but only look upon yourself."

Though the queen was torn between wanting the daughter of her dreams and being revolted by Esmeralda's appearance, her desire proved stronger. "Very well," she said. "I shall allow you to help me." She stepped inside the hovel.

Esmeralda placed a large mirror in the center of her small jumbled room. This mirror was door-like—taller than it was wide. With a surface that fairly sparkled, it was framed by intricately carved wood—carvings of animals, birds, and flowers, crafted so well they seemed to be alive.

Esmeralda sat on one side of this mirror; Isabelle sat on the other, so that the queen gazed only at her own image. Though she had always thought herself beautiful, the mirror's image made her a picture of perfection. This pleased her greatly and she began to relax.

"Very well, my queen," Esmeralda called out from behind the mirror. "Tell me about this daughter you desire."

"My daughter Babette," began Isabelle, "must be the most beautiful girl in Solandia. She must be a child without so much as one blemish or irregularity."

"Why must she be so beautiful?"

"Why," said the queen, "the whole world knows that only the beautiful are happy."

"Ah then," said Esmeralda, "you wish her to be . . . what is the word?"

"*Flawless*," the queen said.

"Very well," said Esmeralda. "My powers can reflect that."

"Then use them," Queen Isabelle commanded.

"So be it!" cried Esmeralda. Then the old hag placed one hand on the top of the mirror, and the other hand on the bottom. She began to squeeze. Instead of shattering, the mirror collapsed into a glassy lump. Esmeralda compressed this lump until it became smaller and smaller. When it became perfectly round, and no bigger than the tip of her small finger, she turned it inside out with her thumbs until it became invisible. She then placed this invisible pill in Queen Isabelle's hands.

"Swallow that," said Esmeralda, "and you shall have a daughter who will appear flawless."

Queen Isabelle hesitated. But when she recalled that the invisible pill was made from the mirror—which had made *her* look so beautiful—she swallowed it down. She waited for something to happen. When nothing did, she became annoyed. "I suppose you now wish me to pay you for something I cannot see?"

"My queen," Esmeralda replied with a bow deep enough to hide the glint in her eye, "who am I to ask anything from such a beautiful and gracious queen? Let me be content in thinking that I've been able to make you happy by helping you have a . . . flawless daughter."

Pleased by such a show of humility, Queen Isabelle flung a halfpenny at the woman's feet and hastened away.

But as the queen went on, she grew uneasy about this Esmeralda and what had transpired. Perhaps the ugly woman had been insincere in her parting words. Perhaps she would talk about the queen's secret visit. Perhaps she would mock her. Who knew what claims the woman might make?

By the time the queen had returned to her palace, she had decided it would be better to banish Esmeralda to the far reaches of the country—the Northern Forest. It was done immediately, but secretly. Not even King Alfredo or the Prime Minister knew about it.

It was not very much later that, with great joy, Queen Isabelle announced she was going to have a baby. The baby was a girl. At least, Queen Isabelle had no doubt the baby was a girl. The moment the child was born, the hardworking and distracted midwife automatically wrapped the baby up in a sweet-smelling blanket, then handed the precious bundle to her mother, the queen. Eagerly wishing to look upon the infant's perfections, the queen pulled aside the blankets and peeked at the baby's face. For a brief moment—a very, *very* brief moment—Queen Isabelle saw *nothing*. However, it was impossible for the queen to believe she had given birth to an *invisible* child. After all, the bundle had a lusty voice. It smelled like a baby. It wiggled and wriggled *just* like a baby. Certainly she had the appetite of a baby. In addition—there could be no denying it—the child had not a single noticeable blemish!

After that one brief frightening moment—when Queen Isabelle had seen *nothing*—the *next* second she was convinced she was looking at the most beautiful baby girl in the world, the very child she had long imagined and always wanted. Of course, she named the child Babette.

With Babette secure in her mother's arms, the midwife stepped outside the delivery room, where King Alfredo was waiting anxiously.

"How is my wife?" he asked.

"Everything went splendidly," said the midwife.

"Wonderful! And the child?"

"A perfect girl."

"Better than wonderful! May I see them?"

The midwife led King Alfredo to the queen's

bedside. There Queen Isabelle said, "Here, husband of mine, is Babette, our new daughter, the future queen of Solandia. Isn't she every bit as beautiful as I desired?"

The king peeked inside the bundle. For just the very small part of a very small second, he saw . . . *nothing.*

"Not so much as one blemish, has she?" said Queen Isabelle.

The king hesitated. "What," he said, "do you like most about her?"

"Exactly what I expected to like," returned the queen. "Her clear blue eyes and blond hair. Just like her mother's."

King Alfredo looked again, and this time he saw the beautiful daughter his wife had so often and vividly described. So he said, "Yes indeed, her eyes *are* quite splendid."

Then he added, "But I confess, it's her delicate nose, and noble forehead—which she gets from *my* side of the family—that *I* admire!"

"You are as perceptive as ever," said the queen.

Because the birth of Princess Babette was important news in the queendom of Solandia, the king went to the Prime Minister and told that wise gentleman how well everything had gone.

The Prime Minister asked, "Is the princess as perfect as her Queen Mother desired?"

"The girl is truly flawless," said King Alfredo. "Just what was wanted." In great detail he described Babette.

The Prime Minister went to the Lord High Information Officer and told *him* the happy news.

"We must send out a proclamation at once," said the Lord High Information Officer. "With," he added, "an appropriate portrait of the princess!"

The Prime Minister agreed.

"Of course," said the Lord High Information Officer, "to do so I must know what Princess Babette looks like."

The Prime Minister provided him with the king's description, adding some details from what he recalled as to the way Queen Isabelle had spoken of her much-desired child.

The Lord High Information Officer went to the Royal Court Artist and asked him to do a portrait of the new princess so every citizen in Solandia would know her likeness.

"Can you describe her to me?" said the Royal Court Artist.

"Of course!" said the Lord High Information Officer, and he gave a fine verbal portrait of Babette—just as *he* had been told.

The Royal Court Artist—who was famous not just for his skill but even more for his ability to create art that satisfied his clients' high ideals—made the portrait. Because there was no one he wished to satisfy more than Queen Isabelle, he painted a stunning picture of the new princess.

When Queen Isabelle saw the portrait, she said, "That's her—exactly!"

Very soon thereafter, a royal proclamation—complete with a portrait of beautiful Princess

Babette—was distributed to every person in Solandia. The citizens, seeing the sweet face of the new princess, their future queen, were very proud. How satisfying that Solandia had a princess without so much as one blemish.

Long live Solandia! Long live Babette the Beautiful!

Of course, when the people actually *saw* Princess Babette, they did experience a brief and puzzling moment of confusion because nothing *seemed* to be there. Nothing to worry about! All they had to do was glance at the proclamation portrait to tell them *exactly* what Babette looked like. Besides, the image they saw was indeed *perfect*.

One other thing of importance happened: Shortly after Babette's birth, Queen Isabelle banished all mirrors from Solandia.

But alas, before Babette was one year old, Queen Isabelle and King Alfredo faded away.

The queen was the first to die. The cause—it was whispered—was madness. Isabelle's symptoms appeared when she took to avoiding all light. Next she bound up her eyes and walked about like a blind person. Her actual death came during the night, when she accidentally fell from the highest point of the castle. It was said she could not see where she was going.

A rumor spread throughout Solandia that the death was somehow connected with the new princess. The Lord High Information Officer, in haste, made it a crime to speak of such a thing. As he explained to the Prime Minister: "The country must protect its image."

As for King Alfredo's death, though the doctors gave medical reasons, it was commonly understood that he died of grief over the loss of his beloved wife. Indeed, his last words were, "*I can no longer see any reason to live.*"

When these sad events transpired, Princess Babette, not yet one year of age, was far too young to take the throne. A queen had to be at least sixteen. So Solandia was ruled—quite properly, it must be said—on her behalf by the Prime Minister.

Years passed. Although Babette remained invisible,

and despite the fact that all mirrors had been banned from the land, the young princess knew exactly what she looked like. She knew this by looking at portraits of herself—which were placed on every wall of every room—throughout the palace. Indeed, the Prime Minister had decreed that a portrait of the princess be placed in every home throughout the entire country of Solandia.

The artists of Solandia were only too happy to comply with the decree, for they loved to paint Babette's picture, readily confessing that the young princess was—after all—the perfect subject.

Did Babette look the same in every portrait? Of course not! Because the talents of the artists differed, so too did the images differ. Still, certain qualities were there. Babette never had a blemish. And—she was always beautiful.

More years passed. Babette's sixteenth birthday approached. In Solandia it was the custom that only after the heir apparent married could she claim the throne as the country's rightful ruler. Of course the choice of a spouse was Babette's, but a choice had to be made. This selection of a husband was to be the most important decision of her young life. Hardly a wonder that the question raging about Solandia was this: Whom among the many suitors would Princess Babette choose to marry?

The court became a beehive of curiosity. Every move Babette made, everything she said, every man she met, was watched and talked about. Only one thing was generally agreed upon: For a princess as beautiful as Babette, only the most handsome man would do.

Shortly before her birthday, the Prime Minister invited Babette's favored suitors—the short list numbered seven—to join her for a week of festivities. Wisely wanting to provide a place for her to make her crucial decision far from the distractions of a court caught up in the frenzy of speculation, the Prime Minister chose a far corner of Solandia— the Northern Forest.

Before Babette left the castle in her carriage, the Prime Minister spoke some words to her: "Choose well, my princess. I have so much faith in your judgment I see no need to come along. Just remember, the eyes of history will be watching you."

With that, Babette went in her carriage, her seven suitors following close behind.

Each day of the following week proved perfect. The weather was lovely. Skies were cobalt blue by day, star bright and crisp by night. "Like Babette," one of the handsome young men noted as he glanced lovingly (so all could see him do so) at the portrait of Babette with which each suitor had been provided.

Babette, meanwhile, met first with one young man and then another. She gossiped idly with one, talked philosophy with another. With a third she went walking. With yet another she went hunting. She did a little of each with each.

"I think I am ready to choose," said Babette to the Royal Trail Master. "I should like to do so dramatically. Have you any suggestions?"

The Royal Trail Master told the princess about a spectacular wild rose he had discovered in the most isolated part of the forest. "It is the most beautiful rose I have ever seen," he informed Babette.

"As pretty as me?"

"Almost."

"Then I will pluck it and present it to the one I have chosen for a husband," said Babette.

Therefore, it was agreed that the entire party would walk through the forest, and then return to waiting coaches. At that point Babette would announce her choice of a husband by giving him the rose. The lucky man would escort her home. All agreed it would be wonderfully romantic and very picturesque.

With soldiers to guard against any mishaps, the party worked its way deep into the forest. But no matter where they all looked, the rose could not be found.

"How annoying," said Babette. "Still, I must make my choice."

When the Royal Trail Master announced it was time to go back to the coaches, a tremor of excitement passed through the crowd. Babette was about to make her decision.

At that moment Babette, remembering the Prime Minister's stern admonition to make her choice with care, called the Royal Trail Master and said, "I need just a few more moments of privacy to make my decision. I shall go for a stroll. Perhaps I'll come upon that beautiful rose."

"Maybe it would be best for me to stay," said the Trail Master.

"No, no," Babette replied. "I require only a short time. I can catch up easily."

Accordingly, the Trail Master waved everybody on. Babette remained. Alone, she clasped her hands and closed her eyes, and began to think very hard about her crucial decision.

While meditating deeply, she heard someone's footsteps. An indignant Babette opened her eyes.

Staring fixedly at her was a twisted old woman. The woman's face was haggard. Her hair was sparse and gray. Her hands were gnarled, and ribboned with veins. Upon her frail shoulders lay a tattered blue-and-green shawl. Babette thought her very ugly.

After a moment of alarm, Babette regained her composure and said, "Who are you? And what are you doing here?"

To which the woman responded, "Who are you to speak so rudely to me?"

"I am Babette, Royal Princess of Solandia."

"Are you?"

"Can you not tell just by looking at me?" Babette returned, annoyed with the rudeness of the woman.

"Perhaps you are what you say," the old woman said, "but perhaps you are not. I cannot tell because I cannot *see* you."

"What nonsense!" Babette replied. "You are talking to *me*. I am talking to *you*."

"I certainly hear you," the woman said. "But all I see is a suit, gloves, a hat, and boots. I don't see a *person*."

"Are you so blind that you don't see my *face*?"

"Be assured I'm not blind, but I don't see your face."

"But it's right here!" Babette cried, pulling off one of her gloves and touching a finger to her own nose. "What do you think I'm touching?"

"I have no idea!" the old woman exclaimed. "What's more, you have no hand, either. Are you, perhaps, a ghost?"

"I am the Royal Princess of Solandia!" cried Babette, stamping her foot with vexation. "Who are you?"

"My name is Esmeralda."

At that moment, the Royal Trail Master, concerned that Babette was overdue, had come back with soldiers. When he saw the princess talking to someone, he stopped.

Though Babette saw the Trail Master and soldiers approach, she continued to give her attention to the woman. "Are you aware," Babette said to the old woman, "that you have insulted me?"

"I beg your pardon," said Esmeralda. "I can tell you only what I see or—in this case—do not see."

"I want this woman arrested!" Babette demanded. "She has offended me grossly!"

It was but a moment's work for the soldiers to take the old woman into custody.

"Bring her to the castle prison!" Babette commanded.

That, too, was done, and in moments the Royal Trail Master and Babette were alone.

"Did the old woman hurt you, Princess?"

Babette was about to say no. Instead she said, "Do I look as if I've been hurt?"

The Royal Trail Master studied her carefully.

"No," he said. "Not as far as I can see."

"What about my face?"

"To me," replied the Royal Trail Master, "you look just as you have always looked."

"And what way is that?"

"Without a blemish. Perfect."

"Fine," Babette said. "That proves the woman is mad. We've probably saved her from harming herself. I feel better already. Let's catch up with the others."

When Babette reached the carriage, her suitors

were all lined up, ready for her great decision. Babette, however, could not free her mind from what had just occurred.

"I need a little more time," she announced.

Babette went home, alone in her carriage. Instead of pondering who would be her spouse, she kept thinking about what had happened in the forest. She did not, of course, believe what the old woman had said. Still, she could not get the incident out of her mind.

When Babette arrived at the castle, the Prime Minister hurried to meet her. "Princess, I understand you met with some trouble in the forest."

"A hideous old woman named Esmeralda insulted me." ↟

"Ah, Princess, the world is full of people who do not see things the way they should. Lacking insight, they are blind to the true beauties of the world."

"It was nothing," Babette assured the Prime Minister. Then she asked, "What happened to her?"

"She's in the palace prison awaiting her punishment, which will be set by the Royal High Judge."

"Good," Babette said.

"And you, have you made up your mind about your future husband?" the Prime Minister inquired anxiously.

Babette replied, "I was too distracted and couldn't see my way clear. I'll make my decision tonight."

That night as Babette was preparing for bed, she examined her face in one of the portraits she used as a mirror. Turning to a lady-in-waiting, she asked, "Tell me, what do I look like?"

To this the woman replied, "Why, Princess, you look exactly like your portrait."

"Which one?"

"Your favorite one. The one on your vanity table."

Babette stared at the portrait for a long time. When she got into bed she kept asking herself, "Do I *really* look like that?"

She slept restlessly.

In the morning the Prime Minister came to ask if Babette had chosen her husband.

"Never mind that," Babette replied. "Has that woman I met in the forest been punished yet?"

"The punishment will be announced today. I can assure you she will be banished. You'll never have to set eyes on her again. But you're not worried about her, are you?"

"No," said Babette. "Though she did insult me, perhaps she feels remorse. If she would apologize and admit her mistake, I'd be inclined to pardon her."

"How gracious of you," the Prime Minister said. "And the matter of your husband . . . ?"

"All in good time . . ."

That afternoon Babette was seated in her audience chamber when Esmeralda was ushered in between two soldiers. The old woman's feet were in chains. Her hands were tied. As she approached the throne, she lifted her eyes and gazed at Babette.

"Very well, Esmeralda," Babette said, "when you look upon me, what do you see now?"

"Your clothes," Esmeralda said.

"No more?"

"If I speak the truth you'll imprison me again."

"Take off her chains. Undo her hands," Babette commanded.

It was done.

"You are a free woman," Babette said to Esmeralda. "Tell me what you see."

"Chains do not change my eyes. I still see . . . *nothing.*"

"Tell me the truth!" cried Babette.

"Princess," said the old woman, "I cannot see what I cannot see."

"Everybody else sees me!" cried Babette.

"Princess," said Esmeralda, "the truth is, you are invisible."

"Invisible! What nonsense!"

"What would you say if I could prove it to you?" Esmeralda asked.

"You can't!"

"Then request that a mirror be brought here."

"A what?" asked a puzzled Babette.

"A mirror."

"What is a mirror?"

"It's a device for seeing the truth about yourself."

"More nonsense!" Babette cried with indignation. "It's impossible to see oneself."

To which Esmeralda said only, "It may be difficult to see yourself, but how else can you know the person you truly are?"

Babette laughed at the old woman. "Look about the walls. What do you see?"

Esmeralda gazed at the portraits of Babette that hung everywhere. Then she said, "I see one false face in many different poses."

"You are mocking me!" cried Babette. "I need only look at my portraits to know what I look like. They are art, and the whole world knows art tells the truth. Those faces are *me.*"

Esmeralda looked from the portraits to Babette and back again. "That's as may be," she said, "but I can't see your real face—if you have one."

"Go back to jail!" Babette cried.

Esmeralda was led away.

Alone, Babette was greatly agitated. She paced and fretted, then sent for the Prime Minister.

"Your Highness," he said, "have you—"

Babette interrupted. "Are there such things called mirrors, devices by which one can see oneself?"

"My princess," the Prime Minister said soothingly, "a mirror is an ancient device. Mirrors distort life. Here in Solandia, we are civilized. Mirrors are . . . primitive. We live by the arts. It was your wise mother who banished them from the nation."

"Fetch me a mirror!" Babette demanded.

"Are you dissatisfied by your portraits?" said the Prime Minister. "Would you like a new one painted? We have some wonderful new young artists who can paint whatever you'd like. Besides, all of Solandia is waiting—"

"Fetch me a mirror!"

"I suppose," said the Prime Minister, "there is one in the attic of the Royal Museum, but—"

"Get it!"

After a long search, an old mirror—hardly bigger than her own hand, and covered by a cloth—was brought to Princess Babette.

Babette first gave the mirror to the Prime

Minister. "Look at it," she commanded, "and tell me what you see."

The nervous Prime Minister did as he'd been ordered to do.

"Well, what do you see?"

"A very old man."

Babette gave the mirror to a lady-in-waiting. "What do *you* see?"

"A very nervous woman."

She gave it to a guard. "And you?"

"A very frightened soldier."

"Leave me!" cried Babette. "All of you!"

It was done. Alone, Babette took the mirror and propped it before her on her vanity table. With very great care she combed her hair, patted her cheeks, pouted her lips, then lifted her chin ever so slightly. That was the way her favorite portrait showed her. Only then did Babette reach out and—heart pounding—look into the mirror.

Seeing *nothing,* Babette gave a shriek and collapsed upon the floor.

———

For the remainder of the day, Babette refused to see anyone. Nor would she let anyone see her. Instead she spent hours sitting before the small mirror, staring at her invisibility. How painful it was to admit that she was nothing. Not only did it mean that no one could truly see her, it meant that they had *never* seen her.

Babette tried to convince herself that she was dreaming, ill, going mad. Had not her mother gone mad?

Before Babette was willing to admit the truth—that the old woman was right, and she *was* invisible—she decided on another test. She took down all her portraits from the walls. Then she sent for the Prime Minister.

"Princess," he said, "the entire country is waiting for—"

"Prime Minister," she said, "look at me."

"With pleasure."

"What do you see?" she asked.

As he normally did, the Prime Minister stole a hasty glance at the walls where the portraits of

Princess Babette usually hung. When he saw that they were gone, he gasped, placed a hand over his eyes, and said, "Princess, I've a frightful headache."

"I insist!" Babette cried. "Tell me what I look like!"

"I don't know," he admitted.

"Go away from me," Babette cried. "Send that Esmeralda to me."

"She's gone."

"Gone!"

"For her unspeakable rudeness to you, dear princess, the Royal High Judge banished her."

"Banished? Where?"

"Where you found her. The remote Northern Forest."

"But . . . !"

"She did, however, leave you a note."

"Give it to me!"

The Prime Minister hurried away, and though he himself did not return, he had Esmeralda's note slipped underneath Babette's door. It read:

Babette: If you wish to become visible, first find yourself in a mirror, and then take what you want.

Esmeralda

Though Babette read the note three times, she could make little sense of it. Raging with frustration, she tore it into shreds. For a while she was too agitated to do anything but prowl about her room, pausing now and again to steal glances at the small mirror. Seeing nothing, she moaned and paced some more.

Now and again there was a knocking on the door. A lady-in-waiting or some other member of the court asking permission to enter, to help her, to feed her, to conduct some business—wondering if she had chosen a husband.

Babette ignored them all.

When she could no longer deny her hunger, she did request food, and also requested a box of paints and a paintbrush. When all was delivered, she forgot about eating. Instead she sat before her mirror and, with the brush, painted on her own face.

First she painted the outlines, then her eyes, nose, and mouth. She could see what she had painted in the mirror, but because Babette was no artist, the result was that she looked like a clown with bad makeup.

"I shall take art lessons," Babette told herself. "I'll pay artists to paint on my face every day."

The thought made her sad. The sadness brought tears that trickled down her cheeks, leaving tracks of emptiness through the paint she had just applied. She tried to smooth out the spots. Her face became a blur.

Babette picked up one of the portraits she had removed from the walls. With scissors she cut out the canvas face, punched out holes for her eyes, attached string to the mask she had made, and placed the image over her face.

When she looked in the mirror, she saw herself as she had always looked before. The canvas mask, however, was hot and sticky. What's more, with the mask in place she could not eat or scratch her nose. It was hard for her to breathe. Stymied to the point of fury, Babette tore off the mask and cut it up into tiny bits.

All that night Babette lay upon her bed, weeping. How she wished she had never met Esmeralda! That made her recall the message that had been left:

Babette: If you wish to become visible, first find yourself in a mirror, and then take what you want.

Esmeralda

"Ah," Babette said to herself with a sigh, "if only I knew how! If only I could talk to Esmeralda and ask her advice." She resolved to find the old woman.

It was about two in the morning when Princess Babette slipped down to the castle stables, saddled a fast horse, and set off at a gallop.

Dawn had arrived when Babette reached the Northern Forest, and the place where she had first met Esmeralda. All was still. Babette's horse blew a frosty breath and nervously pawed the ground.

In the not-too-far distance, Babette observed a glow. At first she thought it was the rising sun. When the glow did not move, however, Babette decided to investigate. She began to walk among the forest trees. A chill wind blew into her face. The only sound was her tread upon the ground. She walked on. The glow grew brighter. Now and again sparks of light exploded as if from a spinning diamond. A cool gray mist began to flow down among the tree roots. The mist seemed to be coming from the glow.

Babette stepped into the mist. It eddied about her ankles like flowing water. She walked through it, moving toward its glowing source. The glow grew brighter.

Babette saw the cause of the glow. Suspended between two great tree trunks was a gigantic mirror. The mirror was taller than it was wide—like a door—and was framed by wood that had been intricately carved. These carvings were of animals and birds, as well as flowers, crafted so well they seemed to be alive. The mirror's surface shimmered and

sparkled even as it reflected the forest that surrounded it.

Though the mirror appeared to be solid, at the
bottom a stream of gray mist flowed out. It was the
same gray mist that ran through the trees, the mist
Babette had followed.

Babette approached the mirror. She stood before it and looked at herself. What she saw was the
clothing she wore, though as before, nothing showed
of her face or hands. But the more she gazed at the
mirror, the more she saw what appeared to be a
multitude of shadowy faces *within* the mirror itself.
There were hundreds, thousands of these faces, none
very distinct, all drifting like feathers in a gentle
wind.

Babette reached toward the mirror. Her fingers
passed into the mirror itself. She pushed farther
until her arm went in up to the elbow. It was as if
the mirror—or what she thought was the mirror—
was in fact a doorway.

She placed her other hand against the glass. It,
too, went through. Babette stood there, arms

extended into the mirror. Then—her heart pounding—she stepped inside.

Babette found herself in a large room suffused with dusty light. The room contained nothing but mirrored doors complete with hinges and handles. These doors were everywhere—on the walls, the ceiling, the floor—so many doors it was impossible to count them. None were marked, nor was there any indication of what lay behind them.

As Babette stood there, all her movements were reflected in the mirrored doors. It was as if she were in the middle of a kaleidoscope.

"Hello!" she cried.

No answer.

Feeling as though she had entered a trap, Babette reached toward the door she had used to enter the room. It swung open slowly.

Beyond was another room. Babette looked in. The room was full of eyes, millions and millions of them. Each one was a different color, a different shape. Some seemed sad. Others were bright and cheerful. A few blinked. Others stared brazenly.

Some appeared brave, some evasive. A few of the eyes gaped fixedly at her, while some, as if shy, shifted away.

Babette reached out and touched one of the eyes. It winked and fell into the palm of her hand. It lay there gazing up at her. Babette looked back. As she did so, she remembered the message from Esmeralda:

Babette: If you wish to become visible, first find yourself in a mirror, and then take what you want.

Esmeralda

Her hand trembling, Babette lifted the eye to her face and pressed it in. She took away her hand. The eye stayed.

Not sure what she was doing, Babette reached out for another eye, took it into her hand, and then pressed it, too, into her face.

Next she turned and stepped out of the room, back into the central hall. She gazed about into the mirrors. In countless images she saw her new eyes. But when she looked back at the doorway through which she had just come, the eye room behind it had vanished.

Babette went to another door and pulled it open. It was a roomful of thumbs. There were thumbs of all shapes, colors, and sizes. She reached for one and pulled it onto her right hand like the finger of a glove.

She held the thumb up before her eyes—and saw it. With growing excitement, Babette reached for another thumb—only to realize just in time that it was also for a right hand. She had to make sure to get a left one. She found one and slipped it on.

Babette went from room to room, finding that each contained something different: ears here, there elbows. Ankles in this one. Noses in another. Knees, wrists, and thighs—all had their own rooms.

When Babette had finished assembling herself, one door remained shut. What could she have forgotten?

She turned the knob. It was a room full of hearts. She picked a large, passionate one and pressed it into her chest.

Another door materialized. She opened it. Beyond was the forest. She stepped out, and then turned back toward the great mirror. For the first time Babette saw herself as she was—complete.

Of course, what she saw was not perfect. She had been in such a rush! Her left foot was slightly bigger than her right. One earlobe had a crease, the other did not. Her face was not quite symmetrical. What's more, she realized that in her haste she had selected one blue eye and one brown eye. But—she reminded herself—it did not matter. They were now *her* eyes and they could see themselves.

She turned toward her horse. The horse looked up, saw who it was, and nodded.

Babette galloped back home.

Did Babette marry? Did she become queen? Did she live happily ever after? None of that is known. What *is* known is that from that time on,

Babette not only could see herself but liked what she saw. Moreover, the world saw her—*truly* saw her—as she was, as she had made herself.

And from that day on she was called—Babette the Visible.

CURIOUS

"JEFF MARLEY," A TEACHER SAID TO HIM, "don't you *ever* mind your own business?"

Jeff said, "I'm just curious."

"But, do you have to know *everything*?" she asked.

"I thought," said Jeff, "that's what students are supposed to do."

"Curiosity killed the cat."

"Why?" asked Jeff. "What was that cat curious about?"

"Oh, Jeff," said the exasperated teacher, and walked away.

Jeff—twelve years old—lived in Rolerton,

Wisconsin, a town with a population of forty thousand. Locals said it was the perfect place to live. Every Fourth of July the town newspaper, the *Rolerton Observer,* ran an editorial stating that if you wanted to experience the real America, Rolerton was the town to visit.

The town was home to Bevlin Farm Machinery, Universe Plumbing Fixtures, the Duckworth Regional Medical Center, Luther Junior College, and the Rolerton Astros, a minor-league baseball team. The original team sponsors were the people who owned the Universe Plumbing Company. They picked the name *Astros* hoping folks would make a connection between *Universe Plumbing* and *Astros.* No one did.

The Astros played in the Midwestern League. Teams came from midsized towns in Illinois, Wisconsin, Minnesota, and Iowa. Most players were right out of college. The season began on Memorial Day. Labor Day saw its end.

The team played in Rolerton Park. It had a perfectly symmetrical field with emerald green grass that looked especially good at night when the arc lights came on. Owned by the town, which maintained it, the park had comfortable wooden seats in open stands. Dugouts were clean. There was a concrete field house, with locker rooms for the two teams and the umpires. The Astros uniforms were bright gray with purple trim, the numbers and the name *Astros* in old-timey letters. Most games started at 7:00 P.M. There were lots of special games, such as Fan Appreciation Night, Kids Night, and Helmet Night. The young ballplayers—if they weren't talking to the high school girls—were always willing to give autographs.

General admission was two bucks. Kids got in for one dollar, though some kids snuck in by way of the right-field bleachers. No one seemed to mind. Two more bucks got you a hot dog and a soda. The hot dogs were plump, the sauerkraut was sour, the mustard plentiful. Fifty cents for some pink cotton candy. Or, you could hang out behind the low center-field fence in hopes that someone would hit a home run. Shag a ball, and you kept it.

Though Jeff liked baseball—he played on a Little

League team—what he really loved about the Astros games was the team mascot. The mascot was known as the Alien.

This Alien was a bulbous bright green creature covered with red polka dots. He had a stubby spiked tail and huge claw-hands with ten fingers on *each* hand, which, being rubbery, bent in all different directions. His face—perhaps a third of his whole body length—was long and narrow, with two large, round blue eyes, which gave him a quizzical look. The creature also had a long pointy nose—carrot-like—the end of which lit up red when one of the Astros did something unusual, like make a good catch, a classy putout, or an error.

The Alien's mouth was purple, large, and perfectly round, giving him a perpetual look of surprise. Two red horns sprouted from his head. When his nose lit up, so did the horns.

Jeff was really curious about the Alien. There was nothing in Rolerton like him. He'd do things like follow behind players, imitating any quirky walks with mocking perfection. If the umpire called an out against an Astro, the Alien would call the player safe, his stubby arms spread wide, nose and horns flashing furiously. Sometimes he ran the bases backward or made fun of the umpires or coaches. Or he would pretend to faint—falling backward— at exciting moments. The Alien posed for pictures with anyone, hugging pretty girls, playfully kicking boys on their butts.

If, during a game, the crowd roared, Jeff was probably not paying attention: He'd have been watching the Alien do a somersault, horns and nose brightly lit. Jeff had seen plenty of mascots for professional teams on TV. Every team in America seemed to have one. But the Astros' Alien, according to Jeff, was the best. Of course, Jeff understood that the Alien was a *costume,* which he supposed was made from foam rubber. That meant *somebody* was *inside* the foam rubber. The more Jeff watched the Alien's funny, mocking ways, the more he wanted to know who the person was inside. As far as Jeff was concerned, it was as if the Alien was making fun of Rolerton. Rolerton people didn't usually act the way it did: mocking things. Of course, people accused Jeff of acting the same way. Maybe that's why he found the Alien so interesting.

Jeff asked his friends if they knew who the person inside the mascot costume was. Not only did they not know—they didn't care. That made Jeff want to know even more.

One night he hung around after a game, waiting at the gate for the players, umpires, and coaches to straggle out. The food vendors, ticket takers, and park staff also left. Since none emerged with horns or a nose that lit up, Jeff could only assume that the Alien was *one* of the people who had already come out. But *which* one? His curiosity grew.

The next day, after the game was over, Jeff waited till everybody had gone home. When the last person came out of the park—an old guy who started locking up the gates—Jeff went up to him.

"Excuse me, sir," he said.

The man looked around. "Hey, kid, it's late. Your parents know where you are?"

"Yes, sir, they do. I'm going home right now. But I was just wondering: Did the Alien come out yet?"

"*Who?*"

"You know, the mascot. The Alien."

"Oh, *him*. Everybody's gone. I suppose he has, too."

"Do you know who he is?"

The man thought a moment, and then shrugged. "Now that you mention it, I don't. Hey, my job is to make sure everyone is gone and things are locked tight. And they are. So I guess that guy is gone, too. Unless it's a different person each night."

"I don't think so," said Jeff. "He's always funny in the same way."

"Funny?" said the man. "Ask me, I think he's just rude. But no, I don't know who he is." That said, the old guy drove off in a pickup, calling, "Better get yourself home, boy!"

The following day, Jeff got to the ballpark early. The Astros, being the local team, arrived in ones and twos. The Iowa City Jayhawks came in an old school bus. Any number of other people arrived, too. Jeff studied them all but did not have a hint as to whom the Alien might be.

"Excuse me, please," he said to one guy who seemed the right size. "Are you the Alien?"

"Who?"

"You know, the mascot."

"Are you kidding?"

When a man in a suit arrived—he looked important—Jeff went up to him. "Excuse me, sir, do you know if the Alien has arrived?"

"Who?"

"The mascot. The guy in the green suit."

"Oh, him? Kid, to tell you the truth, I'm the general manager of the Astros. If it were up to me, I wouldn't have him around. Sort of offensive. But the town seems to enjoy him. Least, they pay his salary. So, no, I've got no idea who he is."

Jeff bought a ticket. Because he was so early, he wandered among the empty seats, and made his way down toward the field, where the Jayhawks were taking batting practice. The gate leading onto the field had been left open. After a moment of nervousness, Jeff went on through, half expecting to be shooed off. When no one paid him any mind, he looked around. The Alien was not there.

Moving along the edge of the playing area, Jeff went toward the field house, which was behind home plate. He kept his eye on the open door.

When he reached it, some of the Astros players were wandering out, carrying gloves and bats. They nodded to Jeff in a friendly way.

"Hey, is the Alien in there?" Jeff asked one of them.

"Nope. Least, not that I saw. You can go on in and look."

Excited, Jeff found himself in a corridor with gray concrete walls and three doors. HOME TEAM and VISITORS were lettered on the doors to the left and right. The middle one was marked OFFICIALS.

Jeff opened the HOME TEAM door into a large bare room with glaring lights. One wall was lined with steel lockers. A long bench sat before it. The floor was littered with clothing. At the far end was another room in which Jeff could see toilet stalls and showers. Nobody was there.

Jeff went to the OFFICIALS room and looked in. It was a smaller version of the HOME TEAM room. Two men in umpire uniforms were straddling a bench, playing cards.

"What's up, kid?"

"I'm looking for the Alien. The guy in the green costume."

"Not here, I'm glad to say," said one of the officials as he slapped down a card with gusto and cried, "Gin!"

"How come no one likes him?" Jeff asked.

The other umpire looked around. "'Cause he's always making fun of people. Like he was better or something."

"Do you know who he is?"

"Nope. Good thing, too. If I did I'd punch him in the nose."

Jeff tried the VISITORS locker room. It was exactly like the HOME TEAM room, even to the discarded clothing on the floor—but still no Alien.

Jeff went back to the playing field. To his surprise the mascot was already out there. Jeff tried to approach him a few times. The Alien kept his distance. Then a town policeman told Jeff to get off the field.

"Do you know who that guy is?" Jeff asked the cop, pointing.

"The mascot? Ask someone from the team. He works for them."

"I thought he worked for the town."

"No way."

During the game Jeff stayed on the third-base side of the field, paying almost no attention to baseball. He spent all his time watching the Alien. As the innings wound down, Jeff's tension mounted. At the top of the ninth, an easy fly ball to the Astros' center fielder provided the third out. The game was over. The Alien ran onto the field and gave the relief pitcher high fives. When the players from both teams lined up and shook hands, the Alien took his place at the end of the Astros' line and acted silly. The players seemed annoyed. Once the handshaking was done, and the players had run across the diamond toward the field house, the Alien went to the two umpires and offered to shake their hands, too. The umpires refused and hurried back to the field house.

The Alien was alone on the field. As Jeff studied him, the creature suddenly turned and stared at Jeff with its enormous eyes. This gave Jeff an odd sensation, as if the Alien was studying him. The next moment the mascot turned away and started toward the field house. Jeff ran after him.

"Hey, kid!"

Jeff stopped.

"No spectators down here." It was a groundskeeper.

"But . . . ," Jeff began. He swung back around to make sure the Alien was still in sight. He had vanished.

"Off the field, kid."

Jeff stared at where the mascot had been. "Where'd the Alien go?"

"Back to Mars, I hope," said the groundskeeper. "Now, beat it."

Jeff ran to the park entrance. He asked five different people if they had seen where the mascot had gone. No one knew.

How can he just disappear? Jeff wondered.

Jeff spent the whole next day trying to figure out a way to get to the Alien. By game time he had an idea. It required an assistant.

"I need some camera help," Jeff said to his friend Dave.

"Is it about the Alien?"

"Yeah."

"You are getting stupid about this," said his friend. "You know, nobody likes him but you. People think he's weird. Like you."

"Just help me," said Jeff as he handed over his cheap camera. "I'll pay your way into the game."

"It's your dime."

Jeff bought two tickets, and the boys went into the park. Game time was in half an hour. The mascot was already on the field, teasing the visiting team, the Duluth Diamondbacks, as they did infield warm-ups.

With Dave right behind, Jeff led the way. He waited till the Alien's back was turned. Then he crept quietly up and tapped him on the shoulder, which was soft and bouncy. "Excuse me," said Jeff.

The Alien spun about, his enormous eyes fixed on Jeff. He started to back away.

"Please!" cried Jeff. "Can I get my picture taken with you?" He gestured toward Dave, who held up the camera.

The Alien paused, then drew closer and threw his arms around Jeff, squeezing tightly. Very tightly.

Suddenly fighting for breath, Jeff pushed the arms off him. For a second the Alien squeezed some more, only to abruptly release the boy.

Gasping for breath, Jeff said, "Who . . . are you . . . *really?*"

Dave clicked the camera. The moment he did, the Alien shoved Jeff away and walked off in his funny fashion.

"Learn anything?" Dave asked.

"No," Jeff admitted. He rubbed his arms. They were sore. He looked at the retreating Alien. *Who is that guy?*

A week passed before Jeff went back to Rolerton Park because the Astros had gone off on a road trip. It was Labor Day weekend, and the last games of the season. If Jeff didn't find out about the Alien soon, he would have to wait until next year.

So he went to the game very early—but not in his usual way. Instead of taking a seat in the stands, he crept *under* the bleachers, which was hard to do. It took a while for Jeff's eyes to adjust to the murkiness of the area with its forest of metal stanchions holding up the seats. The place was littered with old paper cups, bottles—some broken—and discarded food. It stank, too. *It's like a rubbish dump,* Jeff thought. A part of Rolerton one did not see often.

Jeff looked through the bleacher seats onto the field. He was so early he could see a few of the players doing stretches. A groundskeeper was moving around the bases, anchoring bags to their proper places. Jeff read the sign on the low wooden fence that ringed the outfield: TO VISIT AMERICA—VISIT ROLERTON! The Alien wasn't in sight.

Because he was sure he could not be seen, Jeff decided his spot was perfect. The Alien would not know he was there, watching. Jeff kept scanning the field in hopes he would see the mascot emerge from his place—wherever it was.

As Jeff stood there, staring out to the bright field, he heard a soft scraping sound. At first he ignored it, but when it persisted, Jeff looked about, puzzled. With a start, he realized the sound was coming from a pile of discarded hot dog boxes. Or rather, from *under* the boxes.

Jeff watched. The boxes were moving, rising and falling as if something was pushing up from *below*. Then the top box slid to one side, revealing a dark spot beneath. Jeff—his heart beating fast—realized the spot was a *hole* in the ground.

The boxes continued to shift, revealing more of the hole.

In the gloom, Jeff began to see something pink move *within* the hole. He could not tell what it was, though it reminded him of cotton candy—soft, without any particular shape, a blob.

Jeff, realizing he was holding his breath, sucked in some air and stepped back. He told himself he should get out of there. *This is not right.* Even as he had the thought, the upper part of the pink blob began to shape itself into a thin tendril.

Jeff watched, transfixed. The tendril elongated and began to creep—still connected to the main blob—snakelike, over the ground, coiling itself around one of the bleacher stanchions. Having established a grip, the tendril began to ripple until the pink shape began to emerge from the hole—as if it were being pulled. It was only moments before an entire pink mass had emerged—looking, Jeff thought, like a compact, throbbing brain.

Too amazed to move, hardly daring to breathe, a mesmerized Jeff stared at the *thing,* as still another tendril emerged from the mass. That tendril crept down into the hole. Within moments it pulled up a lumpish green mass with red spots. It was, Jeff realized, the Alien *costume.*

Once the oufit was completely out of the ground, the pink tendril pulled down a zipper on the back. The costume fell open, exposing a dark interior. The next moment the whole pink mass slid inside.

Jeff watched as the zipper closed from within. After a moment's pause, the costume trembled, heaved, shook, stood up, and turned around.

"So you finally found me," the Alien said, looking right at Jeff. The voice was thick, clotted.

"Wh—what are you?" Jeff managed to ask.

"A student."

"A *student*? From . . . where?"

"Very far away. What you people call outer space." The Alien's nose and horns lit up.

"What are you . . . doing in that suit?" asked Jeff.

"I use it to study your world."

"*Study?*"

"To observe humans."

"What's that supposed to mean?"

"I'm here to learn about your natural habitat, your way of life. What you consume for food. Your social activities. That sort of thing."

"Why?"

"Curious."

"Are you the only . . . student?"

"The only one in Rolerton," said the Alien. "But

in other—what do you call them? . . . sport parks—there are lots of us."

"You mean," cried Jeff, "all those mascots at all those baseball and football games . . . they have . . . things . . . like you in them?"

"The perfect disguise," said the Alien as his nose lit up. "That way we get to see you at the activity and place that is most important to your lives—your fun and games."

"And you live right *here*?" asked Jeff. "All the time? Under the stands?"

"I don't think Rolerton would be pleased to know about me," said the Alien. "Too much the outsider. Too curious. So I stay. Everything I need is here."

"Everything? What about food? I mean, do you eat this junk?"

"I only eat once a year. Since I'm here just for the season, I'll be gone in a few days. Next season it'll be another student like me. Not that anyone will know about it—except you."

"But . . . what if I tell?" asked Jeff.

"You won't," said the Alien.

"Why?"

"Because," said the Alien, "it's time for my annual meal."

And before Jeff could react, the creature's twenty-fingered hands shot out and grabbed him. Jeff struggled, but the Alien's grip was too tight. The costume zipper opened. Pink tendrils whipped out and wrapped around the boy. In a matter of moments Jeff was pulled into the costume. The zipper slid shut.

The costume bulged here, there, here again, and then ceased to move. Then the Alien went out onto the field for the game.

The Astros won.

Jeff was lost.

Inquiries were made. Rolerton's police chief was puzzled. The town didn't lose too many kids, hardly more than one a year.

Usually it was right around the last day of Rolerton's baseball season. Curious.

The Shoemaker and Old Scratch

THERE ONCE WAS A POOR SHOEMAKER who had little more than the tools of his trade. Not having a place to work, he searched everywhere until he found a very small and dilapidated house. But no sooner did he move in than he discovered the house was overrun with mice. They chewed holes in his leather, drank his glue, and made nests with his thread.

Frustrated, the shoemaker sat upon his front steps to ponder what he could do. After a while a black cat with lemon-colored eyes appeared.

Ah, thought the shoemaker, *the very creature to do the work.*

The shoemaker introduced himself to the cat, explaining that he was a poor maker of shoes who had recently moved into the house only to find it full of mice. "If you get rid of those mice," he said to the cat, "I'll pay you very well."

"How well?" asked the cat.

"Rid my house of mice," said the shoemaker, "and I'll share all my earnings with you."

"How about fifty-fifty?" asked the cat.

"Fifty-fifty," agreed the shoemaker.

"Forever and ever?"

"Forever and ever."

"Deal," said the cat, and she offered a paw, which the shoemaker shook with great solemnity.

The cat went to work. Within a week there was not one mouse to be found in the house.

"Wonderful!" said the shoemaker. "Now I can set down to do my work."

Not only did the shoemaker do that, he soon became quite successful. Each day, however, he waited until he was sure the black cat was sleeping, counted the money he had made, and hid it under the floorboards. He was quite certain the cat did not notice.

One year to the day from when the shoemaker and the cat had made their bargain, the cat announced it was time for her to receive what the shoemaker had promised—half of his earnings.

"Oh, don't be silly," the shoemaker said to the cat. "A cat has no need for money. Besides, you only worked a week. I've worked a whole year. You should be content with a sunny window and the saucer of milk I leave for you each day."

"What about 'forever and ever'?" said the cat.

"Things change," said the shoemaker.

"But a bargain is a bargain," the cat protested.

"Things change," repeated the shoemaker.

The black cat stared up at the shoemaker with her lemon-colored eyes, put up her tail, and went out for a walk. When she returned she did not speak of the matter. In fact, she never spoke to the shoemaker again—not once.

A few days later—it was evening—the shoe-maker returned home after delivering some shoes he had made. All he wished to do was get inside his house, count the money he'd earned, hide it away, and then eat the splendid dinner he'd prepared for himself.

Much to his surprise the front door to his house would not open. He tried the rear door, as well as the windows. Nothing budged. He threw a rock at a window. The rock bounced away. Finally he called inside to the cat to open the door, but the cat did not come.

Frustrated, the shoemaker sat down on the front steps of his house and tried to think of what to do. As he sat there he heard sounds coming from inside. Putting his ear to the door, he listened. The shoe-maker was sure *someone* was inside. He knocked on the door.

"Who's there?" came a voice from within. The shoemaker had never heard such a voice—it rumbled like a barn fire. All the same, he answered, "It's me, the shoemaker."

"What do you want?" the voice demanded.

"What do *I* want?" the shoemaker said. "Why, this is my house. I want to get in."

"You may do so."

"The door won't open."

"I have opened it," said the voice.

The shoemaker put his hand on the door, and this time he was able to unlatch it. He walked in.

Sitting at his table—the remains of the shoemaker's dinner before him—was the strangest person the shoemaker had ever seen. One moment the man was thin. The next moment he was fat. Then he became thin again. When first seen, the man seemed very tall, but within the space of an eyeblink he became quite short. One moment his hair was red, then gray, and then the man became bald. He had a beard. He had no beard. He had a stub nose. No, his nose was long! It was as if the man sitting behind the shoemaker's table was not one man but many men, yet in the end he was but one.

"Who are you?" the shoemaker demanded.

The man behind the table studied the shoemaker

as if to evaluate him. Even as he looked, he changed into a hundred different shapes. But at last he said, "I am the Devil. But if you prefer, you can call me by my more familiar name, 'Old Scratch.'"

"Why are you called Old Scratch?"

"Oh, it's nothing you need bother yourself about, that," said Old Scratch. "Not *now,* anyway."

"Then why do you take on such different shapes?"

"Things change."

"Well then, Old Scratch, why have you come here? And, by the way, where is my cat?"

Old Scratch offered thirteen kinds of smiles, and said, "I have just been playing with your black cat. Lovely creature. Beautiful eyes. We shared your supper. But then we are good friends."

The shoemaker looked about. The cat was asleep on the stranger's lap—or was it his knee, perhaps his shoulder?

"You had no right to do so," said the shoemaker. "That's my dinner, and my cat."

"But you see," said Old Scratch, "my occupation

is to go from house to house throughout the world and pick and choose as best I may."

"Why choose me?"

"Well now," Old Scratch said, "you're not a very important person. You can barely feed yourself and your cat. At least your cat told me you had no money. Is that true?"

"Absolutely."

"By the by, is this cat a partner of yours?"

"Nothing of the kind," said the shoemaker.

"I see," said Old Scratch, as he changed his shape, size, and look. "Well then, since you have nothing worth taking, I thought I should take your cat. Unless, of course, you want her. You could bargain with me. I'm always willing to bargain."

"I've already told you," said the shoemaker, "I've nothing to give. So if you must, take the cat."

"Ah, so that's how you care for old friends!" cried Old Scratch. "Consider my offer a test." As he spoke his head grew long, short, fat, and then thin. "And since you have failed that test, it's *you* I'll take."

The shoemaker became alarmed.

Old Scratch smiled—or was the smile a frown, or a grin, or a pout—and said, "Perhaps you would prefer some kind of bargain which will give you a chance to stay."

"Yes, a bargain!" cried the shoemaker, determined to outwit this changeable fellow.

"I'd like that," said Old Scratch. "You are a maker of shoes. From time to time—considering how much I travel—I need shoes. Would you be willing to try your skills on me?"

What a fool this fellow is, thought the shoemaker. *If there is one thing I can do, it's make shoes.* He said, "That sounds like an excellent idea."

"Here's my deal," said Old Scratch. "Things change, so I shall visit you three times. I shall visit you small. I shall visit you tall. I shall visit you one and all. Each time I come, if you can find a way to put shoes on my feet, I'll not take you. But if ever you can*not* shod me, it's you and your soul I'll take."

The shoemaker, quick as anything, said, "I accept."

The bargain made, Old Scratch vanished.

As for the black cat, she woke up, stretched, and then looked coolly at the shoemaker with her lemon-colored eyes.

Days, months, years passed. After the shoemaker made his bargain with Old Scratch, his fortunes changed much for the better. He began to greatly prosper. He married well. He and his wife had healthy, happy children.

During all this time the shoemaker was not visited by Old Scratch. In fact, so much time went by without his seeing or hearing from him, the shoemaker began to think his bargain was nothing more than a dream. *There's nothing to fear from him!*

As for the black cat—she remained.

One afternoon—it was a hot and lazy summer day—as the shoemaker worked at his bench, a fly began to buzz about his head. Finding it very annoying, the shoemaker tried to brush it away with his hand, but it didn't work. Finally the fly landed right before him on his workbench.

The shoemaker picked up a shoe. He was just about to bring it down on the fly when the insect called out: "Would you kill me, Shoemaker?"

The shoemaker was so startled, he could neither move nor speak.

"Why would you want to kill me?" asked the fly.

"Forgive me," said the shoemaker, thinking, *Where have I heard this voice before?* Then he said, "I didn't stop to consider you might have feelings on the subject."

"Things change," said the fly. "But no one likes to die."

"I apologize," said the shoemaker as he put the shoe he was working on aside.

The fly cocked his head and looked up at the shoemaker. "Does it mean nothing to you that I have no shoes and must go barefoot all the time?"

The shoemaker looked closely at the fly. It was true: The fly had no shoes. At that very moment he realized who the fly was: Old Scratch.

"Yes," said the fly with a chuckle, as if reading the shoemaker's thoughts, "this time, as promised, I am visiting you small. Can you make me shoes?"

The shoemaker remembered his bargain. Knowing he had no choice, he said, "Yes, I can make shoes for you."

"Then do so," said the fly. "And, as you can see, I require three pairs."

The shoemaker set to work. First he measured each of the fly's feet. They were so small he could hardly see what he was doing. Next he cut the necessary leather. What tiny bits they were!

The fly—promising to return when the shoes were done, *if* they were done—flew off.

The shoemaker worked with infinitesimal stitches to make the shoes. Three pairs. It took the shoemaker a year to make them. In addition, his eyes had become so sore as he made the shoes, he could no longer see: He had become blind.

However, no sooner were the shoes complete than the fly returned. "I'm back!" he announced.

The shoemaker fit the shoes to the fly. "There,"

he said with pride, for he had done what he was sure Old Scratch did not think he could do. "I've kept the bargain."

"Things change," said the fly. And he flew off.

As for the black cat, she with the lemon-colored eyes, she slept in a snug and sunny corner, purring blissfully.

Though the shoemaker did not regain his sight, his skills had grown so much while he made the tiny shoes that he no longer *needed* to see. So great was the dexterity and preciseness of his work, he became very famous for making the finest, most delicate of shoes. In addition, he grew quite rich.

More time passed, so much time that the shoemaker began to think his bargain with Old Scratch had been fulfilled.

But one fine fall day—when the air was crisp and cool—while the blind shoemaker was working on a pair of shoes for a duchess, he heard a sound he could not identify. The sound was heavy and rough. Every time it came, the workshop floor shook as if it were atop an earthquake.

Because the shoemaker was blind, he could not see who (or what) was causing such a commotion. "Who's there?" he called.

No reply.

The shoemaker went back to his work thinking that perhaps he had dozed off and had only imagined the sounds. The next moment more crashing and thrashing interrupted him. Now the shoemaker knew something (or someone) *was* there. "Tell me what you are!" he demanded.

Still, no answer.

The shoemaker became angry. He picked up one of his razor-sharp leather cutters, and was about to fling it in the direction from which the sound came, when a voice boomed, "Would you kill me?"

"Who are you?" demanded the shoemaker.

"I am," answered a great voice, "a creature of change. I thought you might know me."

The shoemaker instantly recognized the voice

of Old Scratch. "Forgive me," he said. "I didn't realize it was you."

"Forgive you?" said Old Scratch. "You might have killed me with that sharp cutter of yours. Think of all my friends who would have missed me."

"I'm truly sorry," said the shoemaker, wondering what part of the bargain he would have to fulfill now.

The great voice went on. "It is even worse for me when you consider the great distance I have to go, and yet I have no shoes upon my feet."

"What happened to the ones I made you?"

"Souls and soles both will wear."

"Would you like me to make you new shoes?" asked the shoemaker, knowing very well what the answer would be.

Sure enough the voice replied, "I have visited you small. Now I visit you tall. Yes, I'd like shoes upon my feet. Can you do it? Happily, today my feet number only four."

"I'm sure I can make them," said the shoemaker.

That said, he climbed off his workbench and groped his way to the sound of the voice, feeling for the feet. It was just as Old Scratch had said. He had four feet—but each foot was as big as a house!

When the shoemaker measured the huge feet—it took three days to do so—Old Scratch lumbered off, promising to return when the shoes were done, *if* they were done. The shoemaker purchased all the leather he could find, hundreds and hundreds of yards, and set to work.

As for the black cat, she merely watched.

So big, so heavy were the shoes that the shoemaker made, each took a year to construct. Still, at the end of those four years—working every day, some nights, plus holidays, election days, and one extra leap-year day—the shoemaker made the four shoes. Hardly had they been made when Old Scratch returned. The shoemaker fitted the shoes, and they fit wonderfully well.

Old Scratch thanked the shoemaker for his work. "Well done," he said. "I can almost forgive you for thinking of throwing that cutter at me." Then off he clumped, the ground trembling with every step he took.

Unfortunately, all the shoemaker's hard work making the huge shoes had crippled his hands. They had become so tired, so weak, during the four years, he could hardly cut a piece of paper, let alone leather. He could not even pick up a needle.

Unable to work for himself anymore, the shoemaker had to employ others. No great hardship there. His fame as a skilled shoemaker had spread so widely, he attracted many an apprentice, all of whom he instructed. He did it very well, too. He became richer than he had ever been before. The whole world seemed to desire shoes made under his direction.

So, though the shoemaker was blind and could no longer use his hands, he thought his bargain was not a bad one—and that he had fulfilled his promise. Had he not outdone Old Scratch?

As for the black cat, she with the lemon-colored eyes, she continued to doze her days away in a sunny window.

The shoemaker's life went on. As time passed he quite forgot that his bargain—like all good old bargains that had been bargained since time began—had *three* parts. That did not change.

One bitterly cold winter's day—when he was sitting in his warm shop, listening to the whistling wind outside and feeling quite content to be inside—the shoemaker heard a knock on his door.

"I'm sorry!" called the shoemaker. "I cannot open the door for you. My hands are too weak and I am blind. Please let yourself in."

The door opened. Bone-numbing cold filled the workroom.

"Be so good as to make yourself and your business known!" said the shoemaker.

"My voice should tell you all," came the reply.

In an instant the shoemaker knew then that it was Old Scratch. He knew, too, that Old Scratch had come to visit him for the third and final time. He was not afraid. Had he not outwitted Old Scratch each previous visit? He was sure he could do so again.

"Well then," he said, "what brings you to me this time?"

"No more than we bargained," returned Old Scratch. "Things change. The shoes I've been wearing have traveled so far they've dwindled to nothing."

"Have you thought of retiring?" asked the shoemaker. "That would certainly cheer up many."

"To tell the truth," said Old Scratch, "I'd like to. But I fear retirement would be dull. No, the work I do isn't pleasant, but . . . well, somebody has to do it. Fortunately, I make bargains such as I've made with you. They keep me amused. In fact, I really have no time to chat. I've come to make my last request."

"Request away," said the shoemaker.

"This time," said Old Scratch, "I must have shoes for me as I truly am."

"That's all very well for you to ask," returned the shoemaker. "But how do you expect me to make shoes for you when I can't see what you are?"

"No eye is so blind it cannot see the likes of *me*," said Old Scratch. "Look up!"

The shoemaker looked up. And he *saw* Old

Scratch just as he had been before, a constantly changing man. He was tall, he was short, he was thin and fat. All at once and all the time, he wore a thousand different fashions of every color and hue.

"Yes," the shoemaker said at last, "I can see you. But because of you, my hands have become quite useless. I can make nothing. That's *not* very fair, is it?"

"I suppose not," said Old Scratch. "But I assure you, no old hand is so old it can't feel my presence. Reach out. You'll be able to feel *me*."

The shoemaker did as told. It was as Old Scratch said: He was there, and a very cold *there* at that. "Very well," said the shoemaker. "What must I do for you?"

"Only as you promised," said Old Scratch. "I have visited you small. I have visited you tall. Now I visit you as one and all." So saying, he held out one of his feet. The shoemaker took hold of it. Even as he did the foot changed. First it was wide, then narrow. Then it became short, only to become long. It had five toes. It had sixteen. It turned into a hoof. It had claws. It never stopped changing.

"Now then," said Old Scratch in his most pleasant voice. "Can you make a shoe that fits or not?"

"I think I can," said the shoemaker, trying to gain some time. "But I must work out a plan."

"I have waited long enough," said Old Scratch. His voice was not so pleasant as it had been.

"Three days," said the shoemaker.

"I can spare two," snapped Old Scratch. "I'll be back in forty-eight hours. If you do not have my shoes, then you must come with me." So saying, he went away.

Alone in his shop, the shoemaker thought and thought how he could make shoes for a foot that constantly changed. It seemed impossible. Oh, how he wished he had *not* made this bargain! But he had.

On the second day he began to have an idea, his sole idea. It would have to do.

Fortunately, Old Scratch had restored his vision and healed his hands. That night he labored on a pair of shoes for *himself.* The shoes fit so perfectly, so snugly, that there was *absolutely* no space between foot and leather. They were like a second skin, the best shoes he had ever made. When he had put them on, the exhausted shoemaker lay down to sleep.

As for the black cat, she with the lemon-colored eyes, she just waited, watched, and purred.

When the shoemaker awoke, there, standing before him, was Old Scratch. He was tall, he was short, he was thin and fat—all at once and all the time. "I hope you slept well," said Old Scratch. "You have a distance to go."

"I slept very well indeed, thank you," said the shoemaker. "But I don't plan on going anywhere."

"Do you have my shoes or not?" said Old Scratch. He had many expressions on his face. Not one of them included a smile.

"Almost," said the shoemaker.

"*Almost* is not good enough."

"That's to say," said the shoemaker, "the shoes are made. There is only the question of making them fit."

Old Scratch sneered. "I'm willing to try," he said.

The shoemaker reached down and took off one of his new shoes. He set it before Old Scratch.

"Do you mean to suggest that *this* shoe is for me?" growled Old Scratch.

"I do," said the shoemaker. "Of course, like all good shoes, they will take a little adjusting. Fortunately, you are of a type that can make these adjustments well."

"That's true," said Old Scratch, rather puzzled.

"Very well," said the shoemaker, "try it on."

Old Scratch took up the shoe. Even as he did, his foot grew as large as an elephant's. So though he attempted to put on the shoemaker's shoe, it did not fit. Old Scratch grinned. "I'm afraid you have failed at last. There is no way I can get my foot into this shoe of yours."

"Ah," said the shoemaker. "It must be something caught in the tip of the shoe that prevents you from getting all of your foot in. Try taking it out."

Old Scratch darted a quizzical look at the shoemaker, but nonetheless picked up the shoe and peered inside. "Nothing," he said.

"Search harder," said the shoemaker.

Old Scratch shook the shoe. Nothing fell out.

He reached in. He found nothing. "Empty," he proclaimed.

"You're not looking hard enough," insisted the shoemaker. "You know how skilled I am in my trade. That shoe will fit but only if you are willing to try."

"You're a stupid man after all," Old Scratch snapped. "There is nothing here!"

"Perhaps," said the shoemaker, "you are too big at the moment to reach in. I thought Old Scratch could go anywhere. I guess I was wrong."

Old Scratch was stung by these words. It must be said, he was nothing if not vain. "Of course I can go anywhere!" he cried. "No place is too big or too small for the likes of *me!*" So saying, he made himself small enough to jump into the shoe.

The second he did, the shoemaker grabbed the shoe, pulled it on, and laced it up, trapping Old Scratch against the bottom of the shoe. The shoe fit so tightly, so perfectly, not even Old Scratch could get free.

"Let me out!" he cried.

Instead of answering, the shoemaker opened the

door of his house and began to run as fast as he could. Every time he came down on that foot, he squashed Old Scratch against the bottom of the shoe. Each time he did, Old Scratch shouted, "Ouch! Free me!"

"Not until you release *me* from my bargain," replied the shoemaker.

"Never!" returned Old Scratch, who made up his mind to wait until the shoemaker became tired.

The shoemaker, however, had not run for years and years, so he had lots of energy and strength. Hour after hour, day after day, month after month, he ran.

Seriously pounded, Old Scratch began to think of what he might do to get out of his predicament. It took him a while, but at last he had an idea. He turned himself into an itch.

At first it was a very mild itch—a small, nibbling, wiggling, tickling, crawly sort of an itch. What's more, it settled itself right beneath the shoemaker's smallest toe. At first the shoemaker was not sure what had happened to Old Scratch. He began to think that Old Scratch was gone, that he had out-witted him. That was good, because he had begun to feel a tiny little itch right there beneath his little toe, quite the hardest place of all to scratch.

The shoemaker tried to ignore the itch, hoping it would go away. The itch persisted. It grew worse. It began to crawl up and down along the sole of his foot with a prickly, stickly, tickly, highly irritating sensation that never ceased.

As the shoemaker ran, he tried to stamp his foot down extra hard. The itch stayed. The shoemaker rubbed his itching foot atop his other foot. The itch stayed.

Finally the shoemaker sat down. Was the itch gone? No! It was twice as bad as before. It was as if twenty little fingers with cracked fingernails were plucking, poking, picking, and tickling him.

Desperate, the shoemaker began to take off his shoe. As he did he heard a laugh. As soon as the shoemaker heard the laugh, he realized that the itch was Old Scratch. The shoemaker began to run again.

The itch would not go away. The more the shoemaker refused to scratch, the worse it got. It began to drive him crazy.

He tried to run faster. That did not help. He tried stopping. No better. He plunged his foot in cold water. Nothing. In hot water. Nothing. He ran on ice. He ran on hot coals. Nothing could get rid of the itch!

The shoemaker began to think that if only he could stop for *one* moment—just one small, tiny, infinitesimal moment—and get to that itch, all would be saved.

He had to try.

He stopped. He sat down. He set the foot with its itch before him. He bent over. He unlaced the shoe. He reached down. He counted to ten. One-two-three-four-five-six-seven-eight-nine-ten! Fast as anything, he tipped off his shoe and started to scratch that itch! *Ahhhhh!*

No sooner did the shoemaker do that than Old Scratch jumped out of the shoe, became full size, and dragged the shoemaker away.

"Now you know two things: why I'm called Old Scratch and that some things definitely *don't* change."

But what ever did happen to that black cat, she with the lemon-colored eyes? Why, she was back in the shoemaker's house. When she learned what had happened to the shoemaker—*how* she learned, I don't know—she took from beneath the floorboards one-half—not a penny more, not a penny less—of the money the shoemaker had made. For that was the exact bargain *they* had made so many years ago.

Then the black cat, she with the lemon-colored eyes, went away. Where she went, I don't know.

SIMON

AS AN ONLY CHILD, Simon was indulged by both his mother and father to such a degree that he grew up to be someone who always assumed he was the center of attention. As Simon grew older, he found that he could charm anyone with his bright looks and sharp wit. Though he always managed to avoid doing anything that might be of help or use to his parents, he was quite comfortable in demanding and taking food, clothing, or pleasure—as much as he wished. It didn't matter to him that his parents had little money: No wish or whim of Simon's went unanswered.

As Simon grew into manhood, his demands grew, too. Nothing but the finest would satisfy him. He constantly groomed himself. He dressed lavishly. No surprise that he came to believe people could do no better than admire him.

To the question "What do you want to do with your life?" he would say, "I intend to have the world gaze upon me with admiration and envy."

One of the things Simon had asked for and received was a rifle. From the moment he had the gun in his hands, Simon's chief desire was to become known as the best hunter in the land.

Such were Simon's demands that after a while his parents grew quite poor. When the time came that they could give him no more, Simon became angry. "You are unappreciative parents," he told them. "I must have only the best."

"Simon," said his poor father, "for all I know what you say may be true. But we have nothing left to give you."

To which his mother added: "Your wants and demands have quite ruined us. If you desire more, you must get it elsewhere—and you must get it for yourself."

At these words Simon picked up his rifle and left home without so much as a farewell. Though his mother and father wept to see him go, Simon did not even look back.

Simon journeyed to a village near a great forest. This forest was famous for its wild animals, so Simon decided to become a hunter. He was sure that by selling what he killed, he could earn enough money for his wants and needs.

All Simon's energies now turned to hunting. He was very good at it. It did not take long before the sound of him coming through the forest was enough to bring terror to all the creatures that lived there. They knew that Simon was an excellent shot, that he was greedy, and that he had no mercy.

One day when Simon brought his slaughter to the marketplace, a merchant said, "Simon, you do very well with what you bring me. But let me give you some advice: As great as is the demand for furs and hides, what the rich really want these days are *feathers.* Not *ordinary* feathers, but gloriously colored ones. The kind you can only find in the deepest parts of the forest. A good shot like you should have no trouble with that. Bring me such feathers, and you shall become truly rich!"

That was enough for Simon. Rifle in hand, he set off into the forest and began hunting birds. He shot hundreds of them, stripped them of their plumage, and left their carcasses to rot. As for the feathers, he sold them to the merchant.

As the merchant had promised, Simon soon grew not only rich but also quite famous in that part of the world. He was not satisfied. Wanting everyone to look upon him with awe, he hunted even more.

As Simon brought in more and more wonderful feathers, the demand for them actually grew. Not only were greater quantities in demand, but he was paid higher prices for the most unusual kinds.

One day Simon's merchant friend said, "Simon, it is believed that in the most remote part of the forest lives the Queen-of-All-the-Birds. Her feathers—

so the rumor goes—have the look, the feel of pure gold. She's known as the Golden Bird. Fetch me *her* feathers and you shall be the wealthiest of men. The entire world shall sit up and take notice of you."

His head bursting with visions of wealth and glory, Simon set off in pursuit of the Golden Bird. Though he traveled where few hunters had been, the Golden Bird never passed before his eyes. Simon kept searching.

One day he found himself in the most tangled part of the forest. As he stood looking about, his hunting bag full of feathers, he caught sight of what appeared to be like gold among the trees. Not sure at first that he was seeing correctly, he stealthily approached the glitter.

It *was* a bird but a bird such as he had never seen before. Her beak was blue, sharp, and precise. Her feet were crimson. On her head a jet black crown. But in the rays of light that filtered down among the many-fingered branches, her golden wings sparkled brighter than the sun itself.

The moment Simon saw this bird he was certain she was the Queen-of-All-the-Birds, the Golden Bird herself. Instantly his mind was filled with thoughts of the money and fame he was sure to get after he killed her and stripped her feathers.

Rifle in hand, Simon inched forward. The bird did not seem to notice. She even fluttered down to a closer branch.

Simon crept to within a few feet of the bird. Silently he lifted his rifle and took precise aim at her breast. Just as he was about to squeeze the trigger, the bird turned to him and quite calmly said, "Why do you want to shoot me, Simon?"

Simon, never taking the Golden Bird out of his gun sight, said, "Because I need your feathers."

"You don't *need* them," the bird replied. "In any case, they are not yours to have."

"The world is there for me to take," replied Simon. "When I take what I want, everybody shall take notice of me."

"*Everybody?*" the bird asked.

"*Everybody,*" Simon insisted.

"Then," the bird replied, "I shall help you achieve what you want." With a sudden flutter of her great wings, she sprang upon Simon.

Even as she did, Simon pulled the trigger. The gun fired. The bullet struck true, piercing the Golden Bird's heart. Still, she had sufficient strength to just reach Simon. As she fell, one wing brushed over his face and neck. Then she lay at his feet.

At the same moment, all the leaves from all the trees fell, too, cascading down like the sound of rain— or tears. The forest grew as silent as a cloudless sky.

Simon looked around. Hundreds of birds were sitting on the now leafless branches, gazing mutely at him and the Golden Bird, which lay on the ground before his feet.

Simon merely gazed back. When the birds did nothing, he shrugged, snatched up the dead Golden Bird by the neck, and stuffed her into his hunting bag. Turning his back on the silent, watching birds, Simon started off. His mind was already trying to calculate how much he would get for the golden feathers.

As Simon walked through the forest, he began to hear high-pitched sounds. He paid them no mind. But as the sounds continued, he realized that his name was being called. "Simon!" "Simon!" "Simon!"

Simon stopped. He looked about in search of the people who were calling his name. He saw no humans. It was the birds that were following him.

A little nervous now, Simon continued on.

"Simon!" "Simon!" This time the calls came from directly overhead.

Simon stopped and looked up. The birds he had seen before were gone. Now, barely four feet above him, three black ravens had come to rest upon the branches of a dead tree. Their bright beady eyes, like burning black candles with shiny black flames, were hard focused on Simon.

"Is it a bird or a man?" Simon heard one of the ravens whisper. The voice was high and shrill.

"Ask it," suggested the second raven. Its voice was smooth.

Simon, puzzled that he could understand what the birds were saying to one another, paused to listen.

The third raven hopped along the leafless branch until it dipped and, like an accusing finger, hung a few inches from Simon's face. Cocking its head now this way and now that, the third raven, in a low voice said, "What are you, Simon, bird or man?"

"I am a man, of course," Simon replied.

"And yet," said the first raven, "you speak to us."

To which the second raven added, "What is more, Simon, your neck is like the neck of a bird."

"For *that* matter," the third raven concluded, "so is your head."

Taken aback, Simon put a hand to his neck—to his face. It was just as the ravens had said: From his neck up he was all . . . feathers! What's more, that neck, which had grown to a considerable length, supported an oval-shaped head.

Simon felt his eyes. They were perfectly round and set on either side of his face. Where his nose and mouth had been, he felt a long pointed beak.

Still, when he looked down at himself, the rest of his body remained as it had been—human.

Frightened, Simon dropped his rifle and sack and tried to rub away the feathers.

"We say you are a bird," screamed the ravens. "You are no more a man than we. And you killed the Golden Bird!"

Screaming, the ravens fell upon Simon, pulling and clawing at him. So fierce was the attack that Simon ran off into the forest as fast as he could go. The ravens pursued him so until Simon had to force his way into thick thorny underbrush that was too tangled for them to follow.

The three ravens flew away. As they went, Simon heard them calling his name. "Simon—Simon—Simon." It sounded as if they were laughing.

When he was sure he was safe, Simon crawled out from his hiding place. Having no idea where he was, he began to search for a way out of the forest. All that day and night, he wandered.

At night, by the light of a full moon, he came

upon a pool of water. Thirsty, he paused and bent down. Reflected upon the surface of the pool, mirrorlike, he saw an image of himself. From his neck up—wherever the Golden Bird had touched him with her wing—he had turned into a bird.

Simon stared at his image. At first he tried to tell himself that it was all a dream, that he would wake up and be what he had always been. Even as he tried to convince himself of this, a pack of hunting dogs, howling and baying, leaped out of the bushes and attacked him.

To protect himself, Simon sprang onto a large boulder. The dogs—baying, snapping, and growling—could not reach him. But nonetheless, he was trapped.

Simon was still standing on the rock above the snarling dogs, trying to think how to make his escape, when a group of hunters appeared. They carried rifles and torches. When the hunters saw Simon atop the rock, they stopped short, amazed by his appearance.

After a moment one of the hunters lifted his gun, and was about to fire, when Simon called, "Don't shoot!"

If the hunters had been amazed at the *sight* of Simon, they were even more astonished that the strange creature could *talk*.

"Are you man or bird?" called one of the hunters.

"I am a man!" insisted Simon, relieved to know that though he had understood the talk of birds, he could still speak a human tongue.

"Friend or enemy?" called another hunter.

"Friend to all!" cried Simon.

From somewhere he thought he heard the laughter of the ravens.

"Lift your hands, or wings, or whatever they are!" one of the hunters shouted. "And come down here."

"Call off your dogs," said Simon.

When the dogs were pulled away, Simon climbed down from the rock and approached the hunters. Only then did he realize that one of them had a crown on his head. He was a prince.

"Who are you?" asked the prince, staring with amazement at Simon.

"I am Simon."

"Well then, *what* are you?"

"Through no fault of mine," said Simon, "magic has turned me into what you see."

"I know nothing of magic," said the prince. "But I do know you are the most curious spectacle I have ever seen! You must come with me. Others will enjoy the sight of you."

Simon objected, but the prince would hear no refusal.

Suddenly fearful of what might happen, Simon turned and tried to run away. Two hunters sprang after him, caught him with ease, and held him tightly. They tied Simon's hands behind his back and placed a rope around his neck. Holding this rope, they led him through the woods.

Simon, shocked and hurt to be so badly treated, demanded to be set free. The prince took no interest in what he said. Quite the contrary. Though the hunters kept gawking and talking about him, these men acted as if Simon were incapable of any understanding.

Once, twice, Simon tried to pull on the rope that held him. For his efforts he received a sharp, painful yank. He had to go along.

The hunters reached their camp. Many people were there, men and women of the court. Some were dressed in furs and feathers; Simon recognized these as adornments he had supplied.

Very excited, the courtiers gathered around Simon, looked at him, poked him, treating him as if—marvel though he might be—he were no more than a dumb beast.

Enraged, Simon cursed at them all. This made the people laugh and tease him more, for they found him to be very funny. At last, for the sake of his own pride, Simon decided to say nothing.

When it was time to eat, a great feast was served to all the court. Simon, tied up, could do nothing but watch. No one seemed to consider that he might like to join the festivities. True, from time to time people at the prince's table threw him bits of food. Simon, who was used to eating at a table, at first refused to eat from the ground. But when his hunger grew to be too much, he tried to pick up a few morsels when no one was looking. The rope, however, held him short. He had to stretch his neck forward and peck at the ground. When people noticed, they found his antics amusing, and laughed. Simon stopped eating.

At the feast the prince announced that because he was sure he would find nothing more wonderful than the half-man, half-bird he had caught, his hunt was over. He ordered a cage to be built. Simon was forced inside.

It was not a very big cage. Simon could only sit, and he had to hold the bars to keep his balance. Sometimes a fury took hold of Simon and he shook the bars, causing laughter that made him furious. But there was nothing he could do about it.

The next morning when the prince's party was ready to move on, the cage, with Simon in it, was loaded onto a cart and pulled along with all the other baggage. Simon, in his cage, was displayed as the supreme trophy.

For three days the prince and his party traveled. To Simon's great mortification, he was the center of attraction in every town through which they passed. Because they were going from the country to the city, they went through larger and larger towns. News of the bird-man had gone ahead. Larger and larger crowds came to stare, to cheer, to jeer and poke fun.

Simon glowered at his tormentors. Secretly, he plotted all the malevolent things he would do to them when he got free.

At last the traveling party came to a great city. The prince was led in triumph to his palace through large crowds.

In anticipation of Simon's arrival, an elaborate cage had been built. Simon was forced into it. Then the cage, with him inside, was hoisted into the air and hung like a chandelier in the very center of the court. That way he could be viewed by everyone at every hour.

Sometimes people prodded at him, or banged on the cage to get a reaction. Occasionally Simon would lose his temper. That made people laugh. He screamed insults at them. More laughter. Though people were at first amused, it did not take long for them to take offense—and then lose interest. His cage was placed in a corner by a window. He was ignored.

Days passed. Simon grew sullen. He would not talk or respond to anything or anybody.

Months went by. Simon had no view of the outside world except through a small window in the palace wall. This window looked out into the sky. The most Simon could see of the world was the changing weather.

One day a great banquet was held in the hall. In his cage Simon listened to the talk, the jokes, the songs. Growing restless, he turned to look through the window. Outside, a storm was raging. As Simon snapped at the occasional bit of food thrown to him, he thought that at least he was being fed, and he was dry and safe.

A small brown sparrow flew into the hall to take refuge from the storm. Exhausted, she rested on the window ledge. The sparrow fluffed out her feathers, shook her head dry, and began to preen her tail. Then she caught sight of Simon sitting in his cage.

Simon, though pretending not to, watched the sparrow eagerly.

The bird took a hop closer and studied Simon with great interest. "What ghastly weather!" she chirped.

Simon, grateful for a little friendly conversation, replied, "Yes, it looks it."

"Are you a bird?" the brown sparrow whispered.

Desperate for sympathy, Simon pressed against the bars of his cage, as close to the sparrow as possible. "I was a man," he replied. "But I was turned, partly, into a bird. Now I'm nothing but a creature in a cage for people to stare at and make fun of."

The sparrow settled down. "How did you come to be the way you are?" she asked

Simon told the sparrow how he had hunted

birds and sold their feathers. But then one day he had shot a most unusual bird and—

The sparrow rose up, her beak snapping with anger. "So *you* are the one who shot our Golden Queen!" she cried with fury. "You deserve all the punishment you have. I'd rather be out in the cold storm than warm inside with you." So saying, the sparrow turned and flew out the window.

Simon could only wish that he, too, could fly into the storm.

Two years went by. The prince, who had once prized Simon as his most curious possession, came to be interested in other things. The cage was moved from the central court to a distant room.

As much as Simon hated being looked upon and made fun of, he found his isolation worse. He had nothing to gaze upon but empty walls.

Occasionally the prince would come by and show Simon to a visitor. Desperate for company, Simon would snap his beak and do tricks, anything to keep the visitors a little longer.

The prince was not amused. He called Simon a vain creature and made a point of *not* staying long. His visits grew fewer, then stopped altogether.

Days went by without Simon seeing anyone.

At length the prince decided that keeping Simon was more trouble than it was worth. He came to Simon's cage and opened the door.

"Come out," said the prince. "No one is interested in looking at you anymore. You've become common. It's time for you to go."

An astonished Simon could hardly believe his ears. He thought the prince was simply playing a trick on him, and refused to leave. The prince had Simon yanked from the cage and unceremoniously thrown out of the palace—from the back door.

For the first time in two years, Simon was free. He was elated—at first. His moment of joy was brief. As he stood against the palace door, trying to think of what to do, a group of children found him. They made fun of him, called him names.

In a fury Simon bent down, picked up a stone, and threw it. His arm was weak. The stone fell short. The children laughed and mocked him all the more.

Simon ran away. As the day wore on, Simon began to feel a pain in his stomach that he knew was hunger. With anger and shock, he realized that the prince had put him out without food or money. He was homeless. With nothing to eat, he began to wish he were back in his safe cage.

As he walked along in search of food, he passed an open-air café. Stomach growling, he stopped and watched people eat.

Someone complained about his staring. The manager came out and tried to shoo him away.

"I only want something to eat," Simon begged.

"Do you think you get food for nothing?" replied the manager. "One has to work for it. Or is your brain as small as most birds'?"

"Please!" cried Simon. "It's just that I've not worked in an ordinary way. I've been on exhibition for the prince. I'm willing to do anything for food."

"Ah," said the manager. "You've led a soft life. But I have a kind heart. I'll make you an offer. With that long beak of yours, you should be good at picking up bits the way your fellow birds do. People are always leaving crumbs where they eat. Crumbs attract rats, and I hate rats. You can pick up the crumbs. My place will be clean, and you'll get something to eat."

Simon was revolted by the suggestion. He started to turn away.

"Where else are you going to get food?" asked the manager.

Simon, hearing his stomach growl, agreed to take the job.

The manager led Simon into the restaurant through the back way. He gave him a gray apron and placed a silly cap on his head. "You might as well amuse my patrons," he said. He pushed Simon out onto the floor and told him to get busy. "Don't assume you'll have this job forever," he warned. "If you don't work hard, you'll be gone!"

At first Simon hung back against the walls of the restaurant, pecking only at crumbs he found there. The bits of food whetted his appetite. He reached for more and more. The patrons were greatly amused. They began to throw food at him. Simon, unable to resist, gobbled greedily. People laughed.

Within a short time, Simon, in order to encourage the patrons and keep his job, began to perform tricks, jokes, and songs he had heard at the banquet tables of the prince.

This went over well—for a time. But before long the patrons, most of whom came to the café on a regular basis, grew annoyed. They grew tired of the same jokes, the same songs. They began to complain to the manager that the bird-man was a distraction. After a few complaints, Simon was told to leave.

In despair Simon left. Unable to think of any other place to go, he decided to return to his parents and beg for mercy.

For a week Simon traveled. He went through all the cities and towns he had passed on his way to the palace. He traveled by night so he would not be seen. Only when he grew hungry would he emerge into the light of day to do tricks on street corners for bits of bread.

When he came to the edge of his own village, he grew fearful. Ashamed to show himself, he waited until the day grew dark. When darkness came, he made his way through back alleys to his parents' house. He knocked on the door, timidly.

His mother opened the door. His father stood behind her. When they saw the strange creature, they were taken aback.

"May we help you?" his mother asked.

"I am your son, Simon."

The two old people looked at the creature on the doorstep with disbelief. Then they became angry.

"Our Simon," said his father, "was the most handsome of young men. He would dress in nothing but the best. But you, strange creature, your feathers are dirty, your clothing is ragged."

"Anyway," added his mother, "Simon would not come here. This house wasn't good enough for him. He went off to make his fortune, and no doubt has become rich and powerful. No, Simon wouldn't come back here."

"In fact," his father added, "I suspect that he sent you here to mock us!"

So saying, his parents slammed the door shut.

Heartbroken and exhausted, Simon made his way by cover of night into the forest. When he found a soft place beneath a tree, he lay down. He began to wish that he might never rise again.

Just as he was falling asleep, he heard the baying of hunting dogs. Instantly he remembered how he had been captured. He had not the slightest desire to be caught again.

To protect himself, he dashed deeper into the wood, running from the sound. Alas, no matter where he ran, the baying grew louder. First it was on one side of him, then on the other. He was surrounded.

Frantic, Simon plunged about in search of an escape. Suddenly he caught sight of a glimmer of gold springing among the leaves.

He ran forward. There, flitting from branch to branch, was the Golden Bird. In the moonlight he saw her just as he had seen her before—wings aglitter, black crown upon her head, red feet, blue beak sharp and precise.

Simon stood still, amazed to see the bird alive. Had he not killed her? As he was about to call out to her, he saw a hunter break from a thicket. The hunter raised his gun to his shoulder and aimed right at the Golden Bird.

Simon leaped forward. The bullet intended for the Golden Bird struck him. He fell.

The hunter, seeing a human form fall and fearing he had killed a man, turned and fled.

As Simon lay upon the ground dying, the forest became utterly still. He opened his eyes and looked up. The trees were covered with birds, all of which were staring at him. Among them was the Golden Bird. Simon gazed at her. "Is it really you?" he managed to ask. "The one I thought I killed?"

The Golden Bird fluttered down by his side. "Yes, it's me," she replied softly. "And you, are you the one whom all the world was to notice?"

"Yes," he whispered.

"And *did* the whole world take notice?"

After a moment Simon said, "Yes, but there was one who never noticed the world."

"Who was that?"

"Me," said Simon, and he closed his eyes.

In the forest nothing moved.

The Golden Bird swept her wings over Simon's body. As she did, Simon was again transformed. He became a bird—a complete bird—of great majesty. With another sweep of her wings, the Golden Bird brought Simon back to life.

The Golden Bird leaped into the air. And Simon followed, his great wings beating the dark night, flying by her side, free and whole at last.